Fabulous Fathers

"What could we possibly do that would make your grandmother believe we're getting married?"

Unexpectedly, Gabe's face lit up. "Set a wedding date," he said.

Kassandra backed away from him. "Oh, no," she said, shaking her head. "This was only supposed to be a fake engagement. That's going too far in this charade."

"Then we're going to have to act more like an engaged couple. We'll have to hold hands more and hug every once in a while."

Kassandra nodded. "Okay."

"And kiss more often than we've been doing."

Swallowing, she nodded again. "Okay. No problem." She licked her lips. The thought of kissing him more often made her shiver. She was still tingling from the memory of the last kiss they'd shared. Suddenly she was all too aware—the greatest danger in this charade wasn't disappointing Gabe's grandmother, but falling in love with him...for real!

Dear Reader,

What better way for Silhouette Romance to celebrate the holiday season than to celebrate the meaning of family....

You'll love the way a confirmed bachelor becomes a FABULOUS FATHER just in time for the holidays in Susan Meier's *Merry Christmas, Daddy*. And in *Mistletoe Bride*, Linda Varner's HOME FOR THE HOLIDAYS miniseries merrily continues. The ugly duckling who becomes a beautiful swan will touch your heart in *Hometown Wedding* by Elizabeth Lane. Doreen Roberts's *A Mom for Christmas* tells the tale of a little girl's holiday wish, and in Patti Standard's *Family of the Year*, one man, one woman and a bunch of adorable kids form an unexpected family. And finally, *Christmas in July* by Leanna Wilson is what a sexy cowboy offers the struggling single mom he wants for his own.

Silhouette Romance novels make the perfect stocking stuffers—or special treats just for yourself. So enjoy all six irresistible books, and most of all, have a very happy holiday season and a very happy New Year!

Melissa Senate
Senior Editor
Silhouette Romance

Please address questions and book requests to:
Silhouette Reader Service
U.S.: 3010 Walden Ave., P.O. Box 1325, Buffalo, NY 14269
Canadian: P.O. Box 609, Fort Erie, Ont. L2A 5X3

MERRY CHRISTMAS, DADDY

Susan Meier

Silhouette®
R O M A N C E™
Published by Silhouette Books
America's Publisher of Contemporary Romance

For my dad, John Petrunak

 SILHOUETTE BOOKS

ISBN 0-373-19192-8

MERRY CHRISTMAS, DADDY

Copyright © 1996 by Linda Susan Meier

This edition published by arrangement with Harlequin Books S.A.

Printed in U.S.A.

Books by Susan Meier

Silhouette Romance

Stand-in Mom #1022
Temporarily Hers #1109
Wife in Training #1184
Merry Christmas, Daddy #1192

Silhouette Desire

Take the Risk #567

SUSAN MEIER

has been an office manager, the division manager for a charitable organization and a columnist for a local newspaper. Presently, she holds a full-time job at a manufacturing company.

Even though her motto, "The harder you work, the luckier you get," is taped to the wall of her office, Susan firmly believes you have to balance work and play. An avid reader and lousy golfer, she has learned to juggle the demands of her job and family, while still pursuing her writing career and playing golf twice a week.

Dear Reader,

My father always tried to make Christmas magical for us. There were eleven kids in my family, so money was always tight, but somehow, some way, my dad—in cahoots with my mother—always found a way to make every Christmas memorable.

The year that sticks out most in my mind was the year my father worked out of state. He had to be back at work on Christmas, which meant he needed to be on the road right after lunch on Christmas Eve, and wouldn't be able to spend any of the holiday with us—not even to see us open our presents. We were all upset about that because everyone knew Santa brought the gifts around midnight and my dad would be long gone.

It was a cold year, so we'd blocked off the kitchen from the rest of the house with a blanket and gathered around the table for lunch. After we ate, one of my sisters left the kitchen and immediately ran back yelping for joy that Santa had come while we were eating and all our gifts were under the tree. I was astounded. Getting gifts one day early was about the best thing that could happen to an eight-year-old, but to have it happen the very year my dad couldn't be home for Christmas made the whole episode seem downright magical.

We talked about that Christmas for years. Still do, in fact. I think my sister Helen helped my parents set the whole thing up. She won't admit to it though. Neither will my parents. But whatever the explanation, that one Christmas left us with the feeling that Christmas and family are magic. Real or created by someone who loves you, it doesn't matter. Magic is magic.

Merry Christmas!

Susan Mius

Chapter One

When the elevator doors opened, Gabriel Cayne thought he had walked into an ad for blue jeans. Bent before him, encased in prewashed, natural-fit jeans was the most perfect derriere he'd ever seen. The woman unsuccessfully tried to gather groceries as they rolled in all directions down the hall, but Gabe didn't pay too much attention to her dilemma. For this short span of time he had nothing on his mind but enjoying the view. And what a view. The right kind of curves in all the right places.

His vision of perfection lasted three more seconds, then—after snagging a can of green beans—his quarry straightened, and Gabe saw she was his stuffy, conservative neighbor who lived in the apartment across the hall with her two equally stuffy friends. He almost sighed.

He didn't care to run into her on a normal day, but on this cold, rainy December day, after receiving the news his grandmother was dying, he'd rather take his chances in the rain again than have to make small talk.

"Good evening," he mumbled, trying to be polite, anyway.

Pushing her blond hair off her face, she glanced at him. Even in the dim hall light, Gabe could see her eyes were green. Despite their many "encounters" over her contention that he played his stereo too loud, his parties lasted too long and his friends made too much noise, he'd never noticed them before.

"Good evening," she mumbled, then she bent again, grabbed a jar of mayonnaise and set it along the wall by her door since her shopping bag was so wet it had disintegrated.

Looking down the corridor, Gabe saw her groceries had traveled the whole way to 3C. Though his key was two millimeters away from his lock, the gentleman in him couldn't leave without helping her. He set his briefcase beside his apartment door, placed his wet trench coat on top of it, then strode down the hall as he said, "I'll get these."

But Kassandra wished he wouldn't. Really wished he wouldn't. Not on the day she'd discovered one of her roommates had eloped. Not on the day the engine in her car had caught fire. And not a week before her second roommate was transferring to Boston. She wasn't in the mood to have to be friendly to the six-foot-three playboy from across the hall, no matter how good he looked in his striking black suit....

Or maybe *because* of how good he looked in his striking black suit. The expensive suit—tailored to fit his perfect body—personified everything she disliked about him. He had a flawless life—an easy life. Since he ran his family's company, he not only didn't have to worry about money, but he could do anything he wanted, including have parties until all hours any day of the week. Every time he had a party, Kassandra's baby, Candy, cried all night.

And when Candy didn't sleep, neither did Kassandra . . . and then she'd miss school the next day.

It was no wonder she found it so hard to be nice to him.

"Here you go," he said, striding toward her, holding an odd assortment of canned spaghetti and soups, most of them with cartoon characters on the labels. Her food choices seemed odd to Gabe. Almost odd enough to tease her about. That is, if she had been someone with whom he actually wanted to speak. He made a move to give her the cans, saw her hands were full and looked at her.

Great! Now she was going to have to let him in. They both stifled a sigh.

Kassandra turned and inserted her key into her lock, and the door gave easily. Standing directly behind her, Gabe noticed that her hair looked almost the color of wheat, and was, in fact, quite pretty. Surprisingly pretty. And sweet-smelling, too.

Deciding that train of thought was ludicrous, Gabe moved away from her hair. He bent down to gather a few more items from the floor. Then he followed Kassandra as she led him through her foyer and into her kitchen.

All the apartments in this reasonably new building were neat as a pin, elegant in a functional sort of way. Gabe had decorated his ultramodern—flashy black lacquer trimmed in gold—from the bedroom to the bath to the kitchen. But Kassandra and her two friends had used a softer touch. Though Gabe couldn't say he would want to live here, he sort of liked her overstuffed floral sofa and chair and the green-and-white leaf pattern incorporated into the all-white kitchen. He knew she couldn't afford this apartment on her own and neither could either of her friends. He'd expected it to be an inexpensive nightmare, decorated with everybody's gaudy taste. Instead, he found they must have compromised....

Which amazed him because Kassandra O'Hara had never tried to compromise with him, only demanded that he tone it down. Twice she'd even called the police on him.

That still rankled, particularly since his family owned the company that owned this building. His parents and grandmother continued to get activity reports from the superintendent. Those reports, brief as they were, had to list any visits by the police. And every time the police came to his apartment, his father called for an explanation. Thirty years old, president of a multinational corporation, and he'd had to answer to his dad for making too much noise.

It was no wonder he found it hard to be nice to her.

"I'll just gather the rest of your groceries," he said, and bolted toward the door. He wasn't sorry he'd stopped to help her, but that didn't mean he wanted to spend an extra minute in her company if he could avoid doing so. The sooner he got this over with, the sooner he could leave.

A few seconds later, he returned with soup, frozen vegetables and a loaf of bread. "Where do you want these?"

She forced a smile. "Oh, just leave them on the table. I'll put them away."

"No, no. I don't mind helping," he assured her, also forcing a smile.

But to Kassandra it sounded as if he would rather be wrestling an alligator than helping her, and she didn't want his help, anyway. She was tired. She had some major problems to think about, and worse, Candy would be here any minute. Kassandra had never tried to hide her eight-month-old daughter from Gabe Cayne, but she'd never gone out of her way to introduce them, either. If Gabe had ever given any thought about Candy, he would put two and two together and figure out Candy was the reason Kassandra always complained about his noise. As president of the company that owned this building, Gabe had the power to alter the building's general lease to exclude children, and that wouldn't just hurt Kassandra, it would hurt other people, as well. As long as Candy wasn't too obvious or too visible, Gabe might never make the connection and no one would have to worry.

"I think I can handle things myself from here," she said, trying hard not to sound like she was kicking him out, though she was. "So, you can leave now."

"Gladly," he said, and pivoted away from her. But just as quickly, he turned to face her again. "You know, you've done nothing but harass me for the past several months. You call me if my stereo gets too loud and call the police almost every time I have a party. It was actually very nice of me to be so considerate of you tonight. The least you could do is appreciate it."

"I appreciate it," Kassandra said, straining for a courteous tone as she stowed her groceries and wished he'd just leave.

"No, you don't," Gabe insisted, and Kassandra's temper began to sizzle. "You don't appreciate anything. Sometimes I think you're nothing but a spoiled brat who has to have everything her way...."

Her temper leaped from sizzling to boiling to bubbling over in about three seconds. "Well, isn't that the pot calling the kettle black," she yelped, spinning to face him. "*You*, Mr. Born-With-a-Silver-Spoon-in-His-Mouth, have no right to call me spoiled or a brat."

"Then how do you justify kicking me out?"

"I'm tired," she said honestly. "But more than that I have problems. Big problems I need to think about. My roommates are gone...or going. Janie eloped last night. Sandy's leaving for Boston next week, which means I'm stuck with six months of a lease I can't afford. Then my car broke down this morning and had to be towed. Unless I find a pot of gold at the end of a rainbow, I won't be able to attend this semester of college—can't afford to," she said, gathering steam as rehashing her problems fueled her anger. "Which is something you wouldn't understand because you don't know the first thing about trouble. You've always had everything handed to you!"

"Oh, really, Miss-High-and-Mighty," he shot back. "Try this on for size. I had to wrangle my family's company away from an overpossessive board of directors. I still have a few enemies on the staff. And my grandmother is dying. *Dying!* My favorite person in the world has terminal cancer and she may not live past Christmas." He didn't even pause for breath, but kept on speaking as he took slow, measured steps toward her.

"And if all of that isn't bad enough," he continued, "I now have to go down to Georgia for Christmas vacation and explain to the woman I love most in the world that I don't have a fiancée."

Though his situation was bad—sad—the last of his tirade struck Kassandra as funny, at the very least out of place with everything else he'd said. She didn't smile, wouldn't smile over something so tragic, but she couldn't stop her retort. "What a pity."

"It is a pity," Gabe angrily said, pacing away from her. "I'd made up a story that I was engaged to make my grandmother happy for the past few months, but now it's backfiring. She called me this afternoon and told me that her only wish before she dies is to meet my fiancée."

If his story hadn't involved a dying grandmother whom he obviously loved, Kassandra knew she might have gloated over the fact that he'd made his own bed and now he had to lie in it. Instead, Kassandra felt more than a stirring of compassion. She cleared her throat and said, "I'm sorry." She paused. "Really sorry."

Gabe was really sorry, too. Not merely sorry for antagonizing her, but also sorry that he'd told her so much. No one, but no one, knew about his made-up fiancée except the people he'd made up the fiancée for—his parents and grandmother. Now Kassandra something-or-another, the grouch from across the hall, knew his deepest, darkest secret.

"I'm sorry, too," Gabe said, rubbing his hand across the back of his neck. "I shouldn't have burdened you with my troubles, but it just hit me like a ton of bricks today and I couldn't seem to stop myself from taking my anger out on you." He paused and caught her gaze. "In fact, that's probably why I yelled at you about not appreciating my help. I'm sorry for that, too."

"That's okay," Kassandra said quietly.

A strange, uncomfortable silence settled over them. They'd never had a civil conversation before, and it appeared to Kassandra that neither one of them knew what to do or say next.

"Is there anything I can do to help?" Kassandra finally asked, filling the awkward pause.

Gabe shook his head. "Not unless you'd like to go to Georgia with me and pretend to be my fiancée through the Christmas season."

The absurdity of the suggestion made Kassandra laugh. They couldn't get along for the five minutes it took to gather her groceries. There was no way they could spend three weeks together—particularly not as two people in love. She almost laughed again. "No, I don't think so."

"Yeah," Gabe agreed. Evidently following her line of thinking about the absurdity of the situation, he smiled. In fact, he smiled *at her*.

She found she rather liked it.

He realized it didn't kill him.

They'd actually made some progress.

Ill at ease, he rubbed his hand across the back of his neck again. "So, your roommates are leaving, huh?"

She nodded, regretting that she'd revealed so much to him. Then she realized it didn't matter. She didn't have a fairy godmother. There was no gold at the end of the rainbow. And she wasn't going to be able to keep this apartment. Period.

"I'll probably be turning in a request to get out of my lease."

"That's too bad," he said, and Kassandra could tell he genuinely meant it. "This is a good building, a safe building."

"I know," she agreed. "That's why I liked living here. To tell you the truth, I'm not quite sure where I'm going to go...." Kassandra trailed off, watching as a curious expression crossed Gabe's face.

He looked her up and down, from her feet to her head, then from her head to her feet.

He smiled wickedly, handsomely. "You know, if you think about this, we could be the answer to each other's problems."

Kassandra shook her head. "I don't think so. Unless you'd be willing to let me live here rent free until I get my degree, there's nothing anyone can do to help me."

"But I *would* be willing to let you live here rent free while you get your degree. I'd even be willing to help you with your other expenses, if you would go to Georgia with me for the holidays."

"Thanks, but no thanks," Kassandra said, thinking distress had driven him just slightly delirious and he didn't realize what he was offering.

"Don't say no so quickly," he insisted, this time sounding as if he were getting a little desperate. "I'm serious about this. Rent and help with your other expenses. Figure out how much money it would take for you to finish school and give me a number. I don't care. I really need this favor."

"You must," Kassandra agreed, overwhelmed by his generosity. "But whether you're serious or not doesn't matter, because I can't do it." First, she knew she couldn't impose on her parents to take care of Candy for the better part of a month. Second, she didn't want to miss Candy's first Christmas. Third, she didn't think Gabe Cayne would appreciate her bringing her daughter on a holiday visit with his family—particularly since she didn't know if Gabe knew Candy existed.

And, fourth, his proposition was just a little too good to be true. She'd been around long enough to know there had to be a catch. There was no way she'd hungrily jump at this chance and make a fool of herself.

"You have to do it," Gabe said. "There is no other way out for you."

"Of course there is," Kassandra argued casually. "I might have to adjust my schedule and put back graduation, but I'll get there."

She set some more things in the refrigerator. Out of the corner of her eye she could see Gabe staring at her, clearly thinking she was crazy. "I know what you're thinking," she told him as she busied herself with storing some canned goods. "That I'm nuts. Well, I have a news flash for you. For every bit as much as you might think I'm crazy to turn down such a lucrative offer, I think you're equally crazy for making it."

"Why?"

"Because people who don't have money are always suspicious of people who offer it so freely." Smiling smugly, she tossed a can into a cupboard. "There's a catch. I know there is, so I'm not buying into this."

"What if I told you there was no catch?" he asked.

"There's always a catch."

"Not this time."

His quietly spoken statement stopped her. "You're kidding? You'd let me live here for eighteen months and you'd shell out enough money to take care of my other expenses?"

"I have money. You need it. And you'd be giving up your holiday. Two-thirds of December and a few days into January. To me it's worth it."

Flabbergasted, she shook her head. "You rich people kill me."

"Why?" he countered. "I'm offering you a simple way out of this and you're too...too..."

"Stupid?" she inquired, her eyebrows raised questioningly.

"Stubborn," he corrected her, "to take it. Why?"

"For a million reasons," she said. "First of all, I don't know you."

"Ah, come on. Everybody in this city knows me, at least by reputation—good reputation, I might add. Even you, if you're honest. In spite of the fact that you think my parties are too loud and too long, you know I'm basically a person of integrity. So, saying you don't know me is no excuse."

What he said was true. She did know him by reputation, but more than that she knew his family. *Everybody* knew his family. They weren't merely pillars of the community. Until a few years ago when they retired in Georgia, they *were* the community. The most generous, most benevolent people in town...

Which made his offer even more than tempting. Knowing the family she'd be visiting were such likable, easygoing people made his offer possible. *Very* possible. Rent and expenses for eighteen months. She could actually quit her job as a waitress. Study full-time. Graduate early.

Suddenly he turned and strode toward the door. "I'll tell you what, since this was a spur-of-the-moment idea, I'm going to give you some time to think about it. I'm leaving in my family's private plane Friday afternoon at two, municipal field. If you're not there, I'll understand." He paused and faced her again. "But if you want to come with me, pack for three weeks."

Kassandra watched the door close behind him, then fell into her chair. She could tell from the way he issued that last order that he expected her to be at that airport at two o'clock on Friday.

He'd made an incredibly generous offer—one she could hardly walk away from—and he knew that.

But, then again, he obviously didn't know about Candy....

Chapter Two

At twenty minutes after two on Friday afternoon, Gabe's plane was fueled and had been moved to the boarding area of the small airstrip. Gabe stood in the biting December wind, arms crossed on his chest, as he studied the parking lot of the municipal field. Kassandra was now late enough for him to officially assume that she wasn't coming and had turned him down.

Which seemed impossible. Short of throwing in a block of Cayne Enterprises stock, Gabe didn't know how he could have made her a better offer. Yet, obviously, his very lucrative, very generous proposition wasn't good enough.

On the verge of giving up, Gabe saw Kassandra jump out of a late-model car someone else was driving. Though Gabe felt a burst of relief, followed by a stirring of guilt since he never thought to offer her a ride to the airport, he didn't want to weaken. Couldn't weaken. This trip had to be on his terms, because this was his family. He couldn't have Kassandra calling the shots, or running the show, or even being smart with him.

Not in front of his family.

Somehow or other, he had to get control of this situation and he had to keep it. And that wasn't going to be easy. Not only had this woman kept him and his noise in line for almost a year, but she'd arrived twenty minutes late, and Gabe had waited for her. She was smart enough to know her own power, and she also had him in a very precarious position. They both knew it. Because of his lie he was at her mercy. But what Kassandra didn't seem to understand was that if she didn't play this part right, there would be no point in taking her to Georgia.

Deciding the best thing to do would be to board the plane and leave her to her own devices with her luggage, so it wasn't so obvious he was watching for her, Gabe stepped onto the first step of the three-stair entry to the streamlined vehicle. He made one quick backward glance to confirm the woman he saw really was Kassandra, then boarded, settling himself in one of the eight seats in the small but roomy craft. He even opened his briefcase and set papers all over the seat beside him so she wouldn't realize he'd waited for her.

But twenty minutes later he was still waiting. Furious now, he tossed the paper he was reading to the seat beside him and was just about to go to the cockpit and tell the pilot to leave, when he saw the pilot walking toward him.

"Mr. Cayne, there's a problem in the terminal that needs your attention."

Gabe looked up at Art Oxford. "*My* attention?" he asked, confused.

"There's a woman claiming you're waiting for her..."

"Now, you know I'm waiting for a woman, Art!" Gabe said, bounding from his seat and starting out of the plane. "You should have just told them to let her through."

"But this woman has—" Art began, but Gabe didn't stay to listen to the end of his sentence. He didn't have time to wait. In the few minutes it would take for the pilot to call to the terminal to tell security to allow Kassandra through,

Gabe could straighten this out himself and probably more satisfactorily.

Storming across the tarmac, Gabe muttered to himself about incompetent people. Everybody had been told to let a five-foot-six blonde through to his plane, yet here he was having to make a personal identification. He bounded through the glass door, strode through the small terminal, burst into the manager's office and nearly knocked Kassandra on her bottom.

Dressed in a black wool coat and fluffy cashmere hat, she didn't look anything like the women Gabe normally dated. She wasn't tall. She wasn't slender. And she certainly wasn't sophisticated. Though, she was cute. Cuddly. Sexy in a sweet kind of way. Unfortunately, she was also holding a baby. A little girl dressed in a one-piece pink winter garment with a bunny embroidered on the front. One shock of black hair peeked from beneath the rim of a pink knit cap. She was sucking on a plastic thing that must have been a modern-day version of a pacifier, though Gabe had never seen one that fit flat against a baby's lips before. The minute Gabe stepped into the room, the kid spit it at him.

It thumped against his chest, then bounced to the floor.

"Hey!" Gabe yelped, jumping away from them. He looked at Kassandra, who appeared sufficiently mortified, but the baby only grinned, held out her arms and said, "Dada."

Beyond angry, beyond confused, beyond everything, Gabe merely looked at Kassandra.

She cleared her throat, then bent to retrieve the pacifier before she turned to the airport manager. "Mr. Byron, could we have a little privacy, please?"

"Sure," Charlie Byron said, rising from his seat. "You want me to take Candy with me?"

Kassandra shook her head negatively, then watched as Charlie left the room, closing the door behind him.

"This is the reason I keep nagging you about your noise," Kassandra said as she shoved the dirty pacifier into an open diaper bag. "I have a daughter."

She paused, waiting for him to respond, but Gabe was so flabbergasted he didn't know what to say. Not only did this explain why she always complained, but it made him feel like a heel for disturbing a baby. Worse, it appeared she'd decided to bring her baby to Georgia. Georgia! To meet his mother, his father and his grandmother!

"This is her first Christmas and I don't want to miss it. Besides, I didn't want to impose on anybody by asking them to watch her for three weeks." Kassandra drew a long breath. "So I decided to bring her along," she added softly, cautiously.

"I see," Gabe said as he slid onto a chair, then covered his face with both hands. He absolutely, positively did not know what to say... or do. Taking this woman and her baby to Georgia wouldn't work. His last-minute attempt to save himself from looking like a liar to his family had failed.

"Look," Kassandra said, obviously becoming annoyed with him. "It isn't as bad as you think. Candy's a baby, not a pet rat. I had a choice. Miss out on this opportunity—which I need—or bring Candy along. I didn't want to lose this chance, so here I am. Now *you* have a choice. Take us as a team or leave us as a team, but as I recall—" she paused until she caught his gaze "—you didn't put any stipulations on your offer. You just told me to show up at the airport."

"*You*," he said, then rose so he could pace. "I told *you* to show up at the airport. Not a package deal. I need one girl, not two. And one of you is a little bit too young for my taste, anyway."

The baby babbled happily, clapping her chubby little hands and staring at Gabe as if he were the Prince of Wales, but Kassandra looked at him as if he were crazy. "I don't *want* to leave her. Three weeks is a long time, and it's her first Christmas. That's a special time. I don't want to miss it."

"No, I suppose not," Gabe muttered. Aside from a few company picnics, he hadn't had much contact with babies before. And this one made him nervous. Oh, she was cute enough, but she also had a very unusual way of looking at him—almost as if she already knew him. He tried to get himself out of Candy's line of vision. But the baby must have thought they were playing some kind of game, because when Gabe moved out of her way, she peeked around her mother's shoulder to find him. When she saw him, she grinned, revealing two teeth trying to sprout from her upper gums. "But even so, I can't take the two of you to meet my family."

"Fine," Kassandra said, and she smiled, albeit half-heartedly. "That's your choice. You can't say I didn't give you an option."

If her voice hadn't quivered with disappointment, Gabe might have thought this was a bizarre scheme to annoy him since she was so good at that. Because her voice had trembled, Gabe knew all this was real. She really did have a baby, and she really did hold out the hope that Gabe would let her take Candy to Georgia with them. He glared at her. "Some option."

She shook her head. "That all depends on how you look at it. If you need a fiancée as bad as you say you do, Gabe, then we're actually better than nothing."

His eyes narrowed, but he knew she was right. Taking this woman and child home for the holiday would be much better than taking no one. If he took no one, he didn't have to admit he'd lied. He could always make up the story that he'd broken up with his fiancée. But then his grandmother would be disappointed. And he didn't want his grandmother to be disappointed—not on her last Christmas. Taking Kassandra would make his grandmother happy.

That's as far as he would allow himself to think for right now. "Okay. You win. Let's go."

Kassandra smiled, and Gabe felt the strangest tightening in his chest. She genuinely was one hell of an attractive woman. Not his type, Gabe reminded himself, but very attractive.

Before he could finish that thought, Kassandra pointed behind Charlie Byron's desk. "Candy's car seat, diaper bag, playpen, swing, high chair and overnight bag are all over there," she said, and watched Gabe's mouth fall open.

"All that for one kid?"

"We left most of her things at home," Kassandra announced casually, though she agreed an eight-month-old was not the perfect traveling companion. Still, it wouldn't do to give Gabe any other way or means to find fault with this situation. Particularly since he hadn't yet thought of the most obvious complication. "You can get those. I'll ask Mr. Byron if he can assign someone to help me get my things from Sandy's car. We should be on our way in ten minutes."

"It'll take me ten minutes to haul this stuff through the terminal," he complained, still staring at the pile of baby paraphernalia stacked in the corner, but Kassandra was already halfway out the door. "Wait a minute," he called after her. "How am I supposed to explain Candy to my grandmother?"

Chapter Three

Kassandra didn't give Gabe an answer to his question because she was just about positive he wouldn't like her answer—at least not until he had a few minutes to adjust to the news she'd already given him. But he didn't press for an explanation. Because Candy began to cry the very second they stepped into the small plane, Gabe pulled some papers from his briefcase and occupied himself by reading while Kassandra rocked Candy to sleep.

Unfortunately, after Candy fell asleep, Gabe continued to read. He even read through the short limousine ride to his parents' home. Candy slept. Gabe read. All in all, everything was going smoothly—much better than Kassandra expected—until they turned into the long, circular driveway, and Kassandra got her first jolt of reality.

They were about to meet Gabe's parents, but he hadn't instructed her on the things she'd need to know to pretend to be his fiancée.

"I think there's no time like the present," Kassandra said, gesturing toward the tastefully luxurious white mansion which was now only about a hundred feet away. "For you to tell me a little bit about yourself and your family. Otherwise, we'll never pull this thing off."

Gabe glanced up from his document. He'd apparently come to the airport straight from work because he was wearing one of his tailored suits. His short black hair was combed in the casual way he wore it to the office, not the slick way he combed it for his parties. Dressed as he was, he appeared capable, smart and strong. Powerful. To look at him, no one would ever guess he was the kind to have loud parties, or date women who looked like rejects from rap videos . . . or do absolutely anything to please his grandmother.

"Won't talking disturb the baby?"

"Well, yes," Kassandra reluctantly agreed. "But even if our talking does awaken her, we still need to put a plan together, figure out what I should say when you introduce me. . . ."

Gabe looked down at his papers again. "At this point, I think it's more important that we don't wake the baby."

Feeling summarily dismissed, Kassandra leaned back on her seat. Prickles of fear danced along her spine, but she ignored them. This was his family. If Gabe was comfortable walking into that great big house without a strategy in place, then so be it.

Without as much as a word of comment, Gabe opened the front door of his family home and, carrying Candy, Kassandra stepped through. It took a minute for her eyes to adjust, but once they had, her brow furrowed. Though the huge white mansion had a bright look from the outside, inside it was gloomy and cold. Dark-stained wainscoting covered the lower half of all the walls, even up the stairway. The upper half had been painted an oppressive green. All of the doors were closed to any rooms visible from the hall, making the foyer seem smaller than it really was. A large crystal chandelier hung from the high ceiling, but it wasn't lit. The only light in the foyer came from candle-shaped wall sconces. Still, though it was dark, the foyer dripped with elegance, beauty and money.

"I'm going to show you to a room," Gabe whispered, directing Kassandra up the long stairway of the front foyer as sleeping Candy nestled into her neck. "So you can put Candy on a bed."

Since the quiet house appeared to be empty, Kassandra breathed a sigh of relief. Giving Gabe the benefit of the doubt, she decided he must have known they would have plenty of time for discussions once they got Candy to a bed. She nodded her agreement with his instructions, and once they were on the second floor Gabe led her down a long hall and to a huge bedroom. But when they were behind the closed doors of the bedroom and Candy had been settled in the center of the double bed, Gabe still didn't say anything.

"Your family has a lovely home," Kassandra said, seeking to start a conversation she hoped would lead him into telling her the things she needed to know.

"Yes. Thank you," Gabe agreed absently.

He used the same tone he'd used when he said good morning in the hall the day after the first time she called the police on him, and Kassandra only stared at him. If she didn't know better, she'd think he had every intention of treating her the same way here as he did in Pennsylvania. "Look, Gabe," she said. "You can't give me the silent treatment for the next three weeks. You brought me down here to make your family think you're engaged—happily," she reminded him. "This charade isn't going to work if you keep treating me as if I have the plague."

"I am not treating you as if you have the plague."

"All right, just a bad case of the flu, then," she said, attempting to lighten the mood enough that he'd relax with her.

"Very funny," he said, though he certainly wasn't laughing. "To you this is just a big joke, and in this case I'm left holding the bag. We're going to fail because I don't know a damned thing about kids and I'm supposed to have been dating you long enough that I would be accustomed to your daughter by now," he said, revealing to Kassandra that he might not have been reading through the ninety-minute plane ride to Georgia, but rather thinking about their predicament and not liking the conclusions he had drawn. He combed his fingers through his thick, dark hair. "Hell, I don't know why I bothered bringing you. Once I saw the baby, I should have realized this wouldn't work."

With that, he turned and stormed to the door. "I'm going to get Candy's things," he said, bounding from the room.

Kassandra dropped to the bed, dispirited. She'd never thought of that. A man engaged to marry a woman *would have* been dating her long enough to know her child. And Gabe didn't know her child.

He was right. They were destined to fail. And it was her fault. If she couldn't come alone, be what he wanted, then she never should have come. He had every right in the world to be angry with her.

"What the hell is wrong with Mr. Cayne?"

Kassandra glanced up and saw a short, white-haired woman standing in the open doorway. She wore a simple gray dress and sensible shoes. She clutched a thick black cane in one hand, but her other hand and arm were weighted down with clean linens. "I said, what the hell is wrong with Mr. Cayne?"

For a full ten seconds, Kassandra sat openmouthed, staring at the woman, not quite sure how to respond. Kassandra might not be a member of the ruling class, but she knew one didn't talk about the family's troubles with the maid.

"Uh, thank you for the linens," Kassandra said, hoping she'd changed the subject.

The woman hobbled to the bed and laid the linens on one corner. As she did, sleeping Candy rolled onto her belly and rubbed her face into the comforter. "Well, what have we here?"

"That's my daughter, Candy," Kassandra said.

"Oh, let me guess," the old woman said. "I'll bet this is why Gabriel Cayne went storming out of here a few minutes ago." Leaning over to get a better look at Candy, she added, "He doesn't like complications in his life. Wants everything to be perfect. I wouldn't worry about what he thinks, though. He can be a real uppity pain in the butt sometimes." She pointed at the towels. "Here, honey, put these towels in the bathroom for me, would you?"

"Sure," Kassandra answered, taking the stack from the bed where the maid had set them. Walking to the bathroom, she realized that though she, herself, wasn't actually saying anything, the maid could be drawing all kinds of conclusions from this conversation, and Kassandra knew she had to nip them in the bud. "Mr. Cayne just wasn't expecting me to bring Candy along," Kassandra explained. "At the last minute, I decided I didn't want to miss Candy's first Christmas. He wasn't angry. We were both simply stressed out from the trip. Not only does Candy have more luggage than six adults, but she cried for most of the plane ride. Candy's not the most wonderful traveling companion," Kassandra added as she walked out of the bathroom.

"Nonsense," the old woman said. "I think she's perfect. Why, look at her," she said, smoothing her gnarled fingers along Candy's feathery hair. "She's adorable."

"Yeah, I think so," Kassandra agreed, gazing at Candy's rosy cheeks and velvety skin. Her hair had been matted into little tufts, and the spot right beside her ear held the imprint of Kassandra's coat button, but in spite of that Candy managed to look beautiful. "It is hard to believe Mr. Cayne doesn't find her as adorable as we do."

The maid looked at Kassandra quizzically. "Do you always call him Mr. Cayne?"

"Not really," Kassandra answered, unwittingly thinking of the hundreds of things she'd called him in the past year, particularly the things she'd called him when he woke Candy with one of his parties. "I'm only trying to be respectful."

"Well, the hell with that," the maid said with a cackle. "You can be honest with me."

Not thinking that a very wise idea, Kassandra glanced at the linens. "Were you going to change the bed?"

"Yeah, but you beat me up here," the maid said, still gazing at Candy who was sleeping soundly. "And now one of us is going to have to hold the little one while the other one works."

"Fair enough," Kassandra agreed, glad to be off the subject of Gabe Cayne. "You hold Candy," she said, motioning the old woman to the rocker by the bay window. "And I'll change the bed."

"I like the way you think," the old woman said, her eyes shining. "I could use a few minutes off my feet."

Kassandra was half tempted to ask the poor thing how long she'd been working for the Caynes and how much longer she'd have to work before she could retire, but she thought the better of that one, too.

"Why don't you tell me where you're from while Gabe's out getting your bags?"

Bags wasn't the half of it. There was an odd assortment of baby things too numerous to mention. She didn't want to think about that any more than she wanted to carry on a personal conversation with a member of the staff, but at this moment the conversation was the lesser of two evils. Besides, the question itself was harmless.

"Pennsylvania."

"You work with Gabe?"

"Not really. Actually, I live in his apartment building."

"I see," the maid said quietly.

Kassandra shook her head. "No, I don't think you do. I didn't start dating him because his company owns the building I live in. I started seeing him because he wanted to see me," she said, realizing how easily a story could be created by using the actual facts. "Things just sort of fell into place after that," she added, deciding that this really was simple. Easy enough that they could pull this off—even with Candy—if Gabe would just loosen up enough to give her a few minutes to prime him for his part.

"No kidding," the maid said, genuinely impressed, then she cackled. "To tell you the truth, I'm surprised the old scrooge brought you with him. He never brings his girlfriends down here. From what I hear, he's ashamed of them. In fact, I'm real surprised he's dating a woman who not only has a brain in her head, she also has enough class to give an old woman a break by making her own bed."

Wide eyed, Kassandra gaped at her. "You shouldn't be talking about him like that."

The maid batted her hands again. "Oh, hell, when something's true I think everybody's got a right to say it. Gabe's a chauvinist," the old woman added candidly. "After seeing one or two of his girlfriends, even you would have to admit he's a chauvinist."

Not wanting to touch this conversation with a ten-foot pole, Kassandra frowned.

The maid gave her a crafty look. "You've seen some of the women he's dated, haven't you?"

Kassandra couldn't help it, she winced.

"Awful, weren't they?"

"No, not awful," Kassandra began, scrambling to think of something positive to say about Gabe to counteract her wince, but she stopped herself. The woman just admitted Gabe never brought a girlfriend to Georgia before. Kassandra was the first. So, the *maid* couldn't know about Gabe's girlfriends.

Just as quickly as Kassandra reasoned that out, she also realized Gabe's grandmother *would* know about his girlfriends, if only because of visits to Pennsylvania. She slumped on the bed. "Oh, God."

As she said the last, the bedroom door swung open. "Judas H. Priest," Gabe said, puffing as he dragged the playpen and swing into the room. "I'm surprised you didn't roll up her bedroom carpeting and bring it along."

He looked at Kassandra and then looked past her and saw his grandmother sitting on the rocker by the window, holding sleeping Candy. "Grandma!"

"Don't you grandma me," The woman said as she motioned for Kassandra to take the baby. "You have about four hours of explaining to do, young man," she added, hoisting herself out of her chair. "What kind of man gets angry with his girlfriend because she doesn't want to miss her baby's first Christmas?"

Taken aback, Gabe glanced at Kassandra. Her eyes had widened, and her face had frozen into a look that said quite clearly she'd fallen for one of his grandmother's traps. Seeing this, Gabe smiled. Two could play this game.

"I wasn't angry that she wanted to spend Candy's first Christmas with her," Gabe explained. "I just didn't want to spoil *your* holiday by having a baby around when we're not used to children."

Before Gabe realized what she was about to do, his grandmother swatted him across the back of his knees with her cane. "Poppycock. Don't try to fool the master. I see what's going on here. If I hadn't already realized you gave poor Kassandra a hard time about bringing Candy, I would have known it when I saw you bring Candy's gear in."

She drew a long, life-sustaining breath, and in that second Gave remembered that this woman who talked a good game was in the final minutes of her final quarter. The whole purpose of this visit was to spend some time with his grandmother before she died. And happy time. The purpose was not to argue or antagonize her. Or beat her at her own game.

"Apologize," she said simply.

Without hesitation or qualm, Gabe turned to Kassandra. "I'm sorry," he said sincerely, and suddenly realized he meant it. Not only had his silent treatment been unfair, but the child sleeping in Kassandra's arms wasn't all that bad. A little noisy, maybe, he thought, remembering the plane ride down, but not bad. "I yelled before I thought," he added, leaning toward her. He brushed his lips across Kassandra's for his grandmother's sake, and though the move had been so unexpected Kassandra hadn't responded at all, Gabe got a surprising little jolt.

Telling himself he was testing this only for his grandmother's sake, he took Candy from Kassandra's arms and laid her on the bed. Then he hooked his hands under Kassandra's elbows and forced her to stand before he went back for another taste of her mouth. Not quick, or without thought, this kiss was long and lingering...and purposeful. The way Gabe had life figured, there was a reason behind everything, and once he uncovered the reason, then the problem had no power over him.

But as he kissed Kassandra with purpose and deliberation, he found himself getting lost, forgetting his purpose and losing his deliberation. There was something about the sweet, spicy taste of her mouth that drew him in until he wasn't thinking anymore, he was only feeling. If his grandmother hadn't cleared her throat, Gabe didn't know how far he would have gone, how lost he would have become.

Trying to get himself out of the situation gracefully, he pulled away, but when he did he saw confusion in Kassandra's eyes that mirrored his own. He also saw a sparkle of desire that he knew mirrored his own, too. Both of which he had to think about.

Clearing his throat, he turned to his grandmother. "So, were you going to make Kassandra dust, too?"

"Well, I figured a chauvinist like you better find a woman who enjoys making a house a home," Gabe's grandmother said. She faced Kassandra. "By the way, I'm Emmalee. You can call me Emma if you wish."

"Thank you," Kassandra responded politely, but, inside, her heart was beating so fast she wondered why no one noticed. She hadn't had an overabundance of boyfriends in her life, but she'd had enough to know that kissing Gabriel Cayne wasn't a normal experience. It was like falling out of an airplane, a rush of excitement followed by several minutes of sheer pleasure. Fortunately, she was wise enough to realize the crash to the ground at the end wasn't worth it.

Emmalee began walking toward the door. "Oh, and Gabe," she said as she slowly made her way out of the room. "I hope you're not planning on sleeping in the same room with the baby," she said pointedly.

Gabe smiled. "Grandma, we are always very careful of Candy's feelings, but I'm also very careful of yours. I know your preferences and this is your house. You do not have to worry. Kassandra and I will respect your wishes."

"Good boy," she said, then hobbled out of the room.

Gabe immediately closed the door behind her. "Well," he said, sighing slightly, as if suddenly uncomfortable around Kassandra. "That's one hurdle out of the way. At least no one will question why we're not sleeping together."

Kassandra cleared her throat. "No, they won't."

"On the plane," Gabe said, "I got a little worried that we might have had to—you know—share the same room for appearances' sake."

"I don't think your grandmother would have liked that."

"I was banking on that, but just in case she might have forced us into the same room as a test of our relationship, I knew we could have worked something out, with me sleeping on the floor or something."

Kassandra nodded. "That would have worked."

"Not that we would have to worry about being in the same room. You can trust me," he hastily assured her, but though Kassandra knew Gabe believed himself to be very dependable, what happened between them when they kissed wasn't as manageable as the very controlled Gabriel Cayne would like to believe.

Still, because their sleeping in the same room wasn't an issue, Kassandra smiled. "Yes, I know I can trust you."

Gabriel smiled, too. He smiled his best, biggest, most wonderful smile as he grabbed the doorknob behind him and began to pull the door open. He was certainly glad he'd convinced her he could be trusted, because that meant he only had to convince himself.

The door bumped his back. Gabe stepped out of its way so he could open it completely and slide behind it. Then he waved slightly as he slipped into the hall. For the first time in his life, he was relieved, very relieved, his grandmother was such a prude, because if he had to spend eight or ten hours in the same room with Kassandra, watching her undress, knowing she was wearing very little only a few feet away from him and on the same bed, and remembering what it felt like to kiss her, neither one of them would be safe.

With those thoughts, he headed toward his room and a very cold shower.

Chapter Four

They were already late for dinner when Gabe knocked on Kassandra's door that evening. She let him in while bouncing into her right shoe and trying to fasten an earring simultaneously.

"This isn't good," he said, glancing at her bathrobe.

"I'm sorry, but Candy slept until a few minutes ago and any wise mother knows you never dress yourself before you dress your baby."

From the playpen, Candy gurgled at him. Though he didn't have a clue about why a wise mother dressed her baby first, Gabe turned to Kassandra and said, "No, I suppose not."

Awkward, he stood in the middle of the room, not exactly sure what to do. He couldn't very well wait for Kassandra in the hall while she put on her clothes—that would be a dead giveaway. Yet he didn't quite feel comfortable waiting in here, either.

Kassandra made his decision for him by stepping into the bathroom to finish dressing. "You know, Gabe," she called,

"I was thinking this afternoon that this charade doesn't have to be all that complicated. When I was talking with your grandmother I discovered that the truth works for us in a lot of places. The only thing is, we need to make up some stories about us dating, how we decided to get engaged, even about how you got to know Candy."

"Okay," Gabe agreed absently, sitting on the bed while he studied the brown-eyed wonder in the playpen. Dressed in a red-and-white striped dress, her dark hair adorned with a red flower which was held in place by a half-inch red elastic ribbon that circled her head, Candy looked cute enough to pose in a magazine.

"I've already told your grandmother we live in the same apartment building."

Gabe smiled. "Did she accuse you of dating me for my money?"

Leaning out of the bathroom, Kassandra peered at him. "Almost. I nipped it in the bud before she could."

"Good girl," Gabe said, then Kassandra slid behind the door, going back to doing the things women do in bathrooms. Gabe looked at Candy again. Patting some sort of bright plastic toy, the baby gurgled loudly, reminding him that Kassandra was right. This situation had some anomalies in it that would have to be covered with stories—maybe more lies.

Resting his elbow on his knee and his chin on his closed fist, Gabe shut his eyes. He didn't like the idea of lying to his parents and grandmother, not one damned bit. But he also didn't have any choice. Because Emma worried that he'd never get married, Gabe had invented the story that he was engaged to ease his grandmother's mind. Now, because it was her dying wish to meet the woman who had stolen his heart, Gabe had to introduce Emma to his fiancée. True, this fiancée was fake, but a fake was better than nothing. And in this case, the fake was also a cover for a lie—a bad lie that started with the best of intentions, but a lie nonetheless. Now he was stuck with the consequences—a semi-toothless gurgle machine. As he thought the last, Gabe opened his eyes and found Candy studying him. When she realized his eyes were open, she smiled broadly, revealing gums and two, maybe three, teeth.

He decided she looked like an eight-month-old, almost bald flapper from the Roaring Twenties.

Her grin widened.

"I was thinking we could just tell your grandmother Candy's the result of another relationship, and leave it at that," Kassandra said from the bathroom, intruding into Gabe's thoughts.

"My parents might buy that," Gabe admitted honestly, "but I'm not sure my grandmother will."

"You're not suggesting that you're going to claim her as your own?" Kassandra asked, stretching out of the bathroom to look at him again. The baby gave him a hopeful look and said, "Da-da."

Feeling strangely hypnotized by the little nymph in the playpen, Gabe rose to pace and broke the spell. "No, I don't want to make the story go that far. We were only supposed to have been dating for four months or so...."

"So you don't have anything to worry about, and we can just keep this simple," Kassandra said, then slid into the bathroom again. "If your grandmother asks about Candy's father, I'll just tell her the truth."

For a good thirty seconds, Gabe stared at the bathroom door, wondering why Kassandra didn't tell *him* the truth. He wasn't really curious in a prying sort of way. Just curious. After all, they had to spend the next three weeks together. It was only fair that he know.

He glanced into the playpen again and Candy grinned at him.

On a whim he reached inside for her. "Come on," Gabe said, pulling her out of the playpen. "I'll just hold you here for a few minutes so you get adjusted to me."

But this baby didn't have any adjusting to do. She willingly went to him, even patted his face as if delighted with the texture of his whiskery stubble. With his hands beneath her arms, resting on her rib cage, Gabe held her in a loose standing position. "Anybody ever tell you you're too friendly?" he asked the happy little girl who gazed up at him dreamily.

"She doesn't know fear yet," Kassandra said from the bathroom. "Give her another month or so, though. From what I've read, she's about to tumble into a shyness phase and I won't be able to leave her with my own parents."

Still staring at Gabe, Candy stuck her hand in her mouth. Gabe couldn't quite figure out what to do with her legs, so he just let her dangle in front of him. Candy didn't seem to mind. The closeness gave her the opportunity to study his face.

"Your parents keep her a lot?" he asked, unable to hide his curiosity any longer, and deciding this was as good a way as any to probe discreetly.

"Always," Kassandra replied from the bathroom. "I couldn't make it without them."

"Actually, I'm surprised you got this far," Gabe said, then realizing she might have taken that the wrong way, Gabe hastened to amend it. "I'm not surprised in a bad way," Gabe quickly assured her. Candy said something that was a cross between a "boo" and a "goo," and when she did a little stream of slobber slipped from her mouth to his jacket sleeve. Knowing he would probably be used to this kind of stuff if he really was dating Kassandra, Gabe didn't react, except to swallow a yelp just dying to leap from his lips.

"I'm surprised in a good way. My God, Kassandra, husband and wife teams sometimes have trouble raising a child. And you're doing it all alone. That's quite an accomplishment."

"You don't know the half of it," Kassandra said, stepping out of the bathroom. Kassandra's red jumpsuit matched her daughter's red-and-white-striped ensemble. Her thick blond hair was down, curving into a loose wave that sat casually on her shoulders. She wore enough makeup to accent her features, but not so much as to look overdone.

Gabe's immediate thought was to tell her she looked beautiful, but he stopped it. In the first place, she wasn't the type of woman he dated. He dated uncomplicated women who wouldn't mind marrying him for his money and then doing exactly what he told them to do for the rest of their lives. And Kassandra was nothing like that. She was a strange combination of sophisticated, smart and conservative. If they dated for real, she'd want to be an equal partner. But they weren't dating for real. They were the kind of people who antagonized each other from across a hall, and that's exactly what they would revert to doing the minute they returned to Pennsylvania. There was no need to get too personal. He bit back his compliment and smiled at her.

"Want to take her?" he asked meekly, holding Candy in front of him as if he were afraid to break her.

"You've got to learn to do this," Kassandra said, then shifted Candy until Gabe was holding her on his arm. "See? Isn't that better?"

"Yes," Gabe agreed. He could smell Kassandra's perfume, and that scent tripped the memory of kissing her. He'd hoped he'd blotted that out of his mind for good, but one whiff of her perfume brought it back full force. He felt those odd, wild impulses again, the ones he'd forgotten from his youth. He felt stirrings and longings that went much further and much deeper than were proper for a man who'd only really known this woman for a few hours. And, thinking about it, he couldn't exactly say he *knew* her because they'd never actually held a real conversation.

"I think you should carry Candy downstairs," Kassandra said, making her way to the door. "You could hand her to me as we step into the dining room, so no one sees that you're not completely comfortable with her, but they'll assume you are because you brought her downstairs."

"Sounds logical," Gabe said, but Kassandra was beating a hasty retreat to the door.

God, he looked wonderful tonight, she thought. She wasn't sure if the proper name for the suit he was wearing was a tuxedo, but she could tell this wasn't the kind of suit a man wore to the office. It was more dressy, more stylish, and so perfectly tailored, he looked incredibly sexy. Thinking about him tripped off the memory of kissing him, and Kassandra knew she was blushing. Blushing! She, a woman who'd had a baby, shouldn't blush over a kiss. And not even a kiss, just the *memory* of a kiss. Good Lord, she was losing her marbles.

To keep her face hidden from Gabe, she led him down the stairway, but he had to direct her to the dining room. Exactly as they'd planned, Gabe handed Candy to Kassandra the minute they stepped into the room, but they hadn't needed to plan that far ahead. As Kassandra took Candy from Gabe's arms, both his parents and his grandmother rose and all three offered to take the child—before they were introduced.

Gabe made quick introductions around the table. His parents were Sam and Loretta, two tall, perfectly groomed, very attractive people in their fifties. His grandmother, of course, was Emmalee, a short, dignified woman—when she wasn't pretending to be the maid.

Once the introductions were completed, it was obvious that Gabe's family was having so much fun just having Candy around, that none of them was concerned about how or why she came into this world.

"Oh, Emma told us you had a baby," Gabe's mother said delightedly. "Isn't she darling, Sam?"

Candy grinned broadly. Kassandra pressed her lips together to hide her own grin. "You're going to spoil her," she said, then laughed lightly.

"Grandparents are for spoiling babies," Gabe's dad announced as he beat the women to Candy and slid her from Kassandra's arms.

"Put her in the high chair, Sam," Loretta instructed, but Sam only smiled and shook his head.

"Babies don't eat salad, so I'll hold her through the first course."

"All right," Loretta reluctantly agreed. "But I get to feed her."

"You feed her the peas and the awful stuff," Emma said. "Then I'll feed her the ice cream and she'll like me best."

"I'm sure she'll like you all equally," Gabe said, pulling out a chair for Kassandra. He took the seat beside her. "God knows, if she can like me, she can like anybody."

"It is a bit of a shock to see you with a baby, Gabe," Loretta said honestly. "It's a pleasant shock, but a shock."

"Not only that," Emmalee interrupted, "but Kassandra's not even Gabe's type. She's not bossy, or snotty, or half naked. I think our prayers have been answered, Loretta."

Loretta took a quick, close look at Kassandra. "Why, Emma, you know, I think you're right."

"I'll thank you both not to talk about me as if I'm not in the room," Gabe muttered.

"We've been doing it since you were Candy's age, Gabe. I hardly think we're going to stop now," Emmalee said. "Pass me a roll.

"Besides, it's true," Emma continued as she tore her roll apart and began to liberally apply butter. "This is the woman we've always wished to find in your apartment when we made our surprise visits to Pennsylvania. In fact, I'm so pleased, I swear I could cry."

Right then and there Gabe knew all the torment he'd suffered over the past four days had been worth it. He also knew he'd do anything he had to do over the next three weeks to keep this charade going. Anything. Absolutely anything.

"That's why I think you should get married while you're here."

If Gabe had been drinking something, he would have spit it across the table. Kassandra, however, reacted beautifully.

"We can't, Emma," she said sweetly, then patted Gabe's hand. Grateful, he flipped his palm up, wrapped his fingers around hers and squeezed lightly. "I still have eighteen months of school."

"Eighteen months of school?" Sam asked as he paced behind Emma's chair, patting Candy's back as Candy noisily patted his cheeks.

"Yes," Kassandra answered. "I'm studying to be a teacher."

"A teacher...?" Gabe said, then realized his mistake. But he was just so surprised. From the way she'd badgered him and thrown ordinance numbers at him, Gabe was sure she was studying to be a lawyer. "Is a very wonderful choice for Kassandra," Gabe finished, covering his faux pas the best he could. "She's very good with children."

"Well, I should say so," Emma scoffed, rising from her chair. Without asking for permission or giving a word of warning, she pulled Candy from Sam's arms. "Just look at how happy and pleasant her baby is." Candy picked that exact moment to lean forward and rub noses with Emma. "And what a darling," Emma cooed. "She's so darned sweet she deserves the name Candy." Abruptly Emma stopped herself. She glanced at Candy, then glanced at Gabe, then back to Candy again.

The room seemed to fall into suspended animation, as Gabe felt the weight of the anticipated question—how to explain Candy to his grandmother. From the look on her face, and the way she kept glancing from Candy to Gabe, Gabe believed she almost expected Candy to be his. Kassandra had given him a logical answer for that. But he wasn't sure telling his grandmother that Candy was the result of another relationship would be quite enough to satisfy her curiosity, or placate her delicate sensibilities. He held his breath, waiting.

"You know, Gabe," Emma said, almost giddy. "She looks exactly like you."

He drew a long breath. "She's not mine, Grandma. Candy's the result of a past relationship of Kassandra's."

"Oh, I don't care," Emma blustered. "What I'm saying is, Candy looks so much like you she'll fit right into your family—once you start one," she added craftily. "You do plan to adopt her?"

"Yes," Gabe said, and gave Kassandra a quick look to see how she was reacting. From the expression on her face, Gabe saw Kassandra wasn't going to contradict him—or rescue him. She was letting him keep the ball. He felt a bead of sweat trickle down the back of his neck.

"Good. A child needs security. Though I'm sure I don't have to explain that to you," Emma added, smiling at Kassandra, who, to her credit, nodded, letting his grandmother have her opinions without argument—whether she agreed or not. Which was a hell of a lot more than he could say for his other girlfriends.

"And I also think it's important that everyone in the family have the same name. So when you adopt her, Gabe, she'll get your last name."

Knowing this idea was really passé, and not knowing Kassandra's feelings on the subject, Gabe held his breath. Still not contradicting, Kassandra only smiled.

"Oh, my goodness," Emma said, then laughed noisily. "I just thought of something else. Once you change her name, she'll be *Candy Cayne*."

"Isn't that adorable!" Loretta gasped.

Sam, Gabe and Kassandra all winced.

"Sounds like a stripper," Sam muttered, shaking his head.

Kassandra said, "All I can picture is Candy getting teased through most of her school years." She turned and smiled at Gabe. "Maybe we'd better give this another thought."

"I think I would," Sam agreed just as the maid arrived with dinner. Emma handed the baby to Loretta, who slid her into her high chair. "I'm more interested in hearing about Kassandra's schooling. Do you go full-time?"

"Part-time. I can't afford to go full-time."

Taking her seat, Emma smiled shrewdly. "All the more reason for you to get married now. Then you'd be able to afford to be full-time because your husband would be responsible for your tuition."

Unexpectedly, Kassandra laughed. "Don't you think that's a little bit inconsistent? I'm getting an education because I want to be my own person. Marrying a man to get my independence is almost paradoxical."

"I say it's common sense," Emma said primly. "In my day..."

Candy let out a yelp, and Loretta, Sam and Emma all jumped to their feet.

"She's just anxious," Kassandra told Loretta with a chuckle. "She's a very healthy eater and a fast eater. She wants you to speed things up."

"Oh, I'm making you mad," Loretta cooed to the baby. "Well, we'll just go faster, then."

Gabe watched the way his mother fawned over Candy, feeding her, tickling her, teasing her, and realized he'd never seen his mother like this. She was so happy she was buoyant.

"Give her a bite of the peas," Sam said, and Gabe switched his attention to his father. He'd also never seen his

father like this. Hell, he didn't even know his father liked
kids....

Actually, he didn't know that anybody liked kids. When
a few of his friends had decided to have children, the only
reason they'd given Gabe was that it was time. Or their wife
wanted kids.

"Don't you worry, honey, I'll feed you fast enough when
I get my turn," Emma piped in, and Gabe sat back on his
chair, astounded.

With one yelp the baby had gotten his grandmother off
the track of marriage, without making her mad. She'd done
it quickly, she'd done it easily, and she'd done it well. Gabe
knew she'd done it well because Emma's full concentration
was devoted to Candy. There wasn't one wedding bell ring-
ing in her head.

Gabe relaxed. This was going to work. He knew it was
going to work. All he had to do was get some private time
with Kassandra tonight so that they could get some stories
straight.

And he knew exactly how to do it.

Chapter Five

"That was a very slick move back there."

Gabe shrugged casually, but he smiled to himself. In spite of the fact that his parents had volunteered to baby-sit Candy tonight—or any night, for that matter—no one could ever accurately predict how his grandmother would react. So he'd set them up. When the baby was squealing with delight at the sounds coming from the talking toy in her playpen, and his parents and grandmother were squealing with delight over Candy, he'd simply announced he was taking Kassandra to the movies.

"I lived with my grandmother for the first twenty-two years of my life. I'm the only person who plays her game as well as she does."

Even in the dim light of his car, Gabe could see Kassandra smile. "She's certainly a schemer."

"Pretending to be the maid is an old trick. I swear she's even worn the same old gray dress every time she's used that scam. If I'd been thinking, I would have realized she'd pull it again today," Gabe said, then took a long breath. "Unfortunately, this whole mess had me a little shell-shocked, so I didn't have all my wits about me. But now I do, and it's time we did some planning of our own."

"Oh, no, you don't," Kassandra said. "You're not taking credit for this."

"Excuse me?"

"I've been trying to get you to plan with me since we turned into your parents' driveway, Gabe. We don't just need a few cover stories, we need some basic, all around, general stories. I don't know anything about your past, you don't know anything about mine. We have to fill each other in so we'll know enough about each other that your parents and grandmother will believe we've been dating for four months."

"That's what I just said."

"Yeah, well, it's what I've been saying every time we've been alone since we've got here. Which just goes to show you pay no attention to me."

Gabe's eyebrows rose with surprise. That was the last thing he expected her to say. The problem wasn't that he didn't pay enough attention to Kassandra, the problem was ever since he'd kissed her he paid *too much* attention to her. Not to what she said, but to how she looked, smelled and felt. That's why he hadn't heard her prodding him into planning. He was too busy being uncontrollably attracted to her. And that was the problem. In fact, it was a *big* problem.

It didn't bother him to be overwhelmingly attracted to a woman. It did, however, bother him to be overwhelmingly attracted to *this* woman. They were opposites. Enemies of a sort. Whatever strange chemistry gripped him, he had to keep it to himself or she'd never let him live it down.

"Okay, I'm sorry," he said, apologizing for something he didn't remember doing—since apologizing was better than admitting he hadn't heard her suggestions because he'd been totally distracted by her. "The point is, we have the whole night ahead of us now. You can tell me your life story, I can tell you mine. And we can keep my parents and grandmother sufficiently impressed until this holiday is over."

"Sounds good to me."

"Good."

"Good."

A strange silence fell over the car, and finally Gabe said, "You start."

She peeked at him. "You start."

"All right," he agreed. "I grew up living with both my parents and my grandparents. So I suppose one could say I was a little bit pampered."

Pausing to think of what to say next, Gabe glanced over and saw she was smiling her little know-it-all smile. "I wasn't horribly spoiled," he said. "Just well cared for."

"You're spoiled, Gabe. Face it. Admit it. It's not a crime. Being spoiled and pampered makes you lucky."

"Yeah, well, whatever spoiling and pampering I might have had flew right out the window when my parents left for Georgia. Ten minutes after my parents and grandmother were in the air, the board of directors had me for lunch." He stopped and laughed derisively. "God, right then and there I found out they'd only been nice to me because of my father and grandmother."

Gabe pulled his car into the parking lot of a small diner. "We can talk here," he said, pointing at the restaurant, which looked like nothing more than a double trailer with a neon sign.

He shoved open his door, and Kassandra decided not to wait for him to open hers. After all, they weren't really dating, just co-conspiring. She wouldn't let herself get accustomed to his politeness, or his fancy car, or the fabulous meals. First, because she'd end up fat as a barrel and lazy, but also because it wasn't going to last. On January 3 she'd be shuffling Candy to her parents' house, back in school and waitressing at a restaurant that looked only slightly better than this one.

Gabe waited for her in front of the car, and they walked into the diner together. They chose a booth in the back, something quiet, and after ordering coffee, Kassandra said, "Was it really that bad when you took over your family's company?"

"I know why you're skeptical," Gabe admitted with a chuckle. "I never would have believed I'd have so much trouble. I mean, I'd known most of these people my whole life. Half had worked with or for me for the six years I'd been in training. I couldn't believe it when I couldn't so much as requisition a pen without getting grilled."

"What happened?"

"I spent the first six months running around, trying to do everything everybody wanted me to do, trying to make everybody happy, and trying to make sure everybody still liked me. Then one day Grandma pulled one of her surprise visits, and one junior executive too many embarrassed me. Without a word, my grandmother went back to Georgia, and I went into the office the next morning spitting nails."

Kassandra couldn't help it, she laughed. "I'll bet that was a sight."

Gabe snickered at the memory. "You better believe it. I figured out I was working so hard to please people who were supposed to be pleasing me that I wasn't steering the company anymore. We weren't losing money—not enough to ruin us anyway. Half the planet would have to be destroyed before Cayne Enterprises would see any real damage. But we weren't growing, either. I had plans and I wanted to implement them. Eventually, I did. But first I had to get back control of the company. I fired three department heads in two hours and gave their jobs to their administrative assistants. I haven't had a problem since."

Kassandra sat back on her bench seat. After studying Gabe a few seconds, she said, "All right, I give up. Why give their jobs to their administrative assistants?"

Gabe smiled a slow, sexy smile. "Just to shake everybody up."

Kassandra's pulse immediately reacted to both his smile and the confident way he said that. She felt the beginning of another blush and prayed her face wasn't as red as she knew it could get. One thing was certain, when Gabe Cayne said he was going to shake things up, he did. Including her. She'd do well to remember how much he could affect her with only a smile. She had to learn to control herself.

"Okay, so I've just told you the beginnings of my life. Now, you tell me yours."

She cleared her throat. "Well, I haven't done anything as auspicious as fire the core staff of a corporate giant. So, we don't have too much ground to cover. I'm the fifth of five kids. I didn't go to college after high school because I didn't have a clue about what I wanted to be and knew my parents couldn't afford to waste money while I hung out at a university to discover myself."

He shrugged. "Makes sense."

"Then one day my boss commented that I was very good, very patient, with the children who came into the diner. We got to talking about how I felt about children and the next thing I knew I'd decided I wanted to teach. The rest, I guess, is history."

For a few seconds, Gabe said nothing, only stared at his coffee. Then he raised his dark brown eyes until he caught her gaze. The look he gave her was part sizzle, part admonition. Gooseflesh sprung up on her forearms. "Candy's not history," he said quietly.

"No, Candy's very much a part of the present and future," Kassandra said, smiling to cover her nervousness.

"She's the most important thing in my life right now. In some respects she's more important than my degree."

"That's good," Gabe said, but he still held her gaze with his soul-searching eyes, and Kassandra knew beyond a shadow of a doubt her answer hadn't pleased him.

"You don't believe me."

He shook his head. "Oh, no, I believe you."

"Then what's wrong?"

"Kassandra, are you going to make me pull this story from you word by word?"

"Oh," Kassandra said, then she glanced down at her coffee. "Well, no." Now that she knew what he was driving at, Kassandra became incredibly uncomfortable. Not because she felt she'd done anything wrong, but because the most noteworthy thing in her life was how she chose to handle being a single mom, while the most noteworthy thing in Gabe's life was gambling with a multibillion-dollar company. And she wasn't even sure that was the most noteworthy thing in his life. For all she knew, through his companies he could be behind the scenes in finding a cure for cancer, or revolutionizing banking through use of personal computers.

"If this is embarrassing, we can save it for another..."

Kassandra shook her head. "It's not embarrassing. It's just life. Part of life. My life. My little, actually very dull life."

For a full thirty seconds, Gabe merely stared at her. He studied her face, her hair, her eyes, the base of her throat. Then he said, "Dull is in the eyes of the beholder." He paused, toying with his spoon. "Let me ask you something. Are you doing what you want to be doing?"

After a moment's honest consideration, she nodded. "Yes."

"Fulfilling all the responsibilities you need to fulfill?"

She nodded again. "Yes."

"Accomplishing goals you want to accomplish?"

This time she smiled. "Every day."

"Then your life's not dull. It's important." He stirred his second cup of coffee. "Tell me about Candy."

His response relaxed her so much she spoke frankly. "I'd been dating Candy's father off and on since high school."

"Eight years?" he said, but it sounded more like a gasp.

She smiled. "At the time it was six. And basically that's why I never married Jeff. If you can date somebody for six years and never once think about marrying him, a baby shouldn't force your hand."

He pondered that, then returned her smile. "No, you're right. You're a hundred percent right. I never looked at it that way."

As he spoke, Kassandra began to feel odd. Not so much as if a bond was being formed, but more like a barrier was crumbling. She was sitting here talking personally, *civilly*, with Gabe Cayne, the man she'd wanted to have arrested ever since Candy had been born. And he was actually agreeing with her. She almost felt as if she'd entered a time warp.

They finished their second cups of coffee happily talking about every detail of their lives they could think of, then left the restaurant. The night air was still warm, the cloudless sky sprinkled with stars. "I wonder what the weather's like in Pennsylvania tonight," she said, laughing.

"Who cares?" Gabe said, and casually draped his arm across her shoulders.

Kassandra immediately stiffened.

"You're going to have to get used to this, Kassie." Instead of letting her go, he pulled her a little closer.

"There's no one around, so I really don't think we need to be doing this stuff."

"Does it bother you that much?"

No. Actually it didn't bother her at all. It felt perfectly natural. Strangely right. Almost wonderfully right. My God, she thought, this time last week, she was ready to hang this man from the nearest tree. Tonight, she hadn't merely enjoyed an evening of conversation, but she'd shared her darkest secret as though he had every right to know. Now she liked having his arm around her.

"I'm getting your door," he said, because by the time Kassandra's thoughts had finished themselves Kassandra and Gabe were already at the car. "No actor would ever attempt Broadway without a few rehearsals, so just think of this as one of ours."

Accepting that logic, Kassandra not only let him open her car door, she acknowledged that he'd have to walk her to her room, if only so anyone listening would hear the right amount of footsteps going in the right directions.

"Which is your room?" she asked softly as they paused by her bedroom door.

"Hang a left at the end of that hall, go to the end of the next hall, and I'm on the right."

"This house sounds more like a maze."

He smiled. "It is a maze."

Now that the evening was over, Gabe wasn't quite sure how to end it. They weren't really dating. They weren't even really friends. Actually, they weren't anything. A kiss was out of line. A handshake seemed absurd. Yet he didn't feel right about just turning and walking away.

Unfortunately, Emmalee knew exactly how the evening should end. She flew out the door of Kassandra's bedroom and almost knocked them over.

"Kiss her," Emma said, then pushed passed them. "And don't you dare go into that room. Remember, I'm watching. I didn't spend the past hour rocking that baby to sleep only to have the two of you wake her."

"Candy had trouble sleeping?" Kassandra asked in alarm.

"No, dear. I just like to rock her. She's going to be spoiled as hell when you take her home," Emma said, then she cackled with glee. But when she stopped laughing, she turned to Gabe. "Well, kiss her already so we can get out of here."

Chapter Six

Gabe knew he didn't hesitate for more than three seconds, but those three seconds felt like an eternity.

He glanced at Kassandra's pink lips just as her tongue darted out and moistened them with a long, slow arch. Then their gazes met and a torrent of sensation washed over Gabe. Lost in her gorgeous green eyes, he felt the excitement of the afternoon's kiss return full force. Even the tips of his toes tingled.

Without a doubt, Gabe realized kissing her again would be like throwing a boulder to a drowning man.

He also knew that if he didn't kiss her—and greedily—his grandmother would think something was wrong.

He set his hands on her shoulders, but quickly remembered that engaged people would be much more intimate, and slid his palms down her shoulder blades, past her ribs, along the neat indentation of her waist, and to the sweet curve of her hips.

Her eyes widened slightly, but to her credit she kept her composure, even taking a short step toward him as he nudged her nearer. As their faces inched closer, they watched each other with an odd combination of curiosity and anticipation. Instinct told him she was waiting for the same thing he was. To see if the excitement of that first kiss was the result of disorientation and shock, or if they really did share some kind of chemistry.

Their lips met tentatively, like the wisp of a feather as it fell to lush grass. Tiny tingles of electricity exploded everywhere their lips touched. He tightened his hold on her waist. She gripped his shoulders as if hanging on for dear life. Thus braced, he drew her closer still, and pressed his mouth firmly against hers. With a small groan, both shut their eyes.

For a full minute, he allowed sensation to numb him. He let the exhilaration of arousal begin. He let his wishes nudge aside common sense as he used his hands to memorize her back, the curve of her hips, her rib cage. He did this partially because his grandmother was watching, and also because he was enjoying this—really enjoying this—and he knew one kiss wouldn't take him so far that he couldn't stop when the time came.

He pulled out of the kiss by slow, deliberate degrees, permitting himself the luxury of one last glide of his hands down the graceful curve of her back, one last taste of her mouth, and one last nibble on her soft, plump lips. Then, he stepped back and swallowed hard.

Well, that was it. Confirmation. The way he saw this the two of them were nothing *but* chemistry.

"Good night," he said, but the words came from a voice that was deep and gruff.

"Good night," she whispered in reply.

"And good night, Mrs. Calabash," Emmalee said, sounding exasperated. "Come along, Gabriel Alan. After that kiss you're going to need a cold shower, but to keep up with three women and a baby at the mall tomorrow you're also going to need a full night's sleep."

Gabe stopped dead in his tracks. "I am *not* going shopping with you."

"Of course you are, dear," Emma said kindly. "Somebody's got to push the stroller."

After their third visit to department store Santas, Gabe was grinding his teeth. Not only was Kassandra enjoying this, but, from the looks of things, that damned kiss last night had meant nothing to her.

Not that it "meant" anything to him, he quickly amended in his thoughts as Emma made a fool of herself trying to get Candy to giggle and his mother's eyes filled with tears at the joy of it all. It was just that Kassandra seemed so calm, so cool, so collected. He'd felt things he hadn't felt since he was a teenager—chemistry the likes of which he figured somehow, some way, deserted a person after the age of twenty-seven or so. Yet she didn't seem to be any worse for the wear. Hell, she could star in a movie, she looked so good.

Not that he was noticing how good she looked in a sexual kind of way. He wasn't. Today he had that end of things pretty much under control. He merely didn't like noticing how good she looked for any reason, sexual or otherwise, because he didn't like her. He didn't *want* to like her. She'd made his life miserable over the past several months. Six days ago, she was the last person in the world he wanted to make conversation with, let alone become friends with, let alone share chemistry with, let alone actually *like*.

She was his arch enemy. She'd called the police on him. Yet here she was being her normal self—not the quiet, sweet girl he'd taken to dinner last night—and she wasn't getting on his nerves the way she was supposed to....

Dammit! He *was* starting to like her!

Frustrated, he jerked the stroller out of the way of three children and their frazzled mother. He chalked up his liking for her to chemistry and proximity, and quickly, mercilessly, dismissed it. *Only two weeks and six days more,* he grumbled to himself, then he could go home and they could officially hate each other again.

"You know, Gabe..." Loretta said as she walked off the Santa platform, straightening Candy's red velvet dress. Instead of her flapper ribbon, Candy wore a fake sprig of holly in her hair, complete with berries. In a curious, chaotic sort of way, she matched the spiral of holly decorating the rail leading to Santa's big chair. "There is one thing that's been puzzling me."

"Where're you going to put all Candy's Santa photos?" he asked, smiling, but hoping his point hit home.

His mother shook her head. "No. I have plenty of places to put these for the holiday, then after New Year's I'll give one to you, one to Kassandra and keep one... Oh, my. Kassandra, dear," Loretta called over her shoulder to Kassandra, who was helping Emma down the three steps that led to the platform. "Do you think your mother would want a picture of Candy with Santa?"

"Yikes!" Kassandra said. "I almost forgot about my mother."

Loretta snagged Gabe's arm. "Let's go find another Santa," she said, leading him in the direction of another department store.

"No. Oh, no," Gabe said, extricating himself from his mother's hold. "*I* am not finding another Santa," he said firmly. "I refuse."

"Okay, fine," Loretta said, smiling pleasantly. "Emma and I will be happy to get another picture of Candy for Kassandra's mother."

Feeling the weight of an anticipated guilt trip, Gabe stood ready.

"We'll meet you and Kassandra back here in about a half an hour," his mother said, smiling sweetly. "That should give you plenty of time to go and speak with Arnold."

"Arnold?"

"Your friend, Arnold Feinburg. You remember. The jeweler."

For a good thirty seconds, Gabe only stared at his mother. "I thought Dad always bought you jewelry for Christmas."

"He does," Loretta said, smiling. Then she did that thing with her eyes that she always did when she wanted Gabe to catch some hidden meaning in her sentence.

Not at all in the mood to play games, Gabe sighed. "Then, what would *I* want to visit Arnold for?"

"Because Loretta and I don't see a diamond on Kassandra's finger. That's why, cheapskate," Emma said, grabbing Kassandra's left hand and waving it in front of Gabe's nose.

This time it was Gabe who said "yikes," but he said it in his thoughts, even as his face broke into a warm smile. "Did it ever occur to either one of you know-it-alls that there might be a good reason I hadn't yet given Kassandra's ring to her?"

"Yeah, it occurred to me right away," Emma said. "If you give it to her for Christmas then you don't have to buy her a real present."

"Grandma, you really know how to take the fun out of a good gift."

"So, you admit you've gotten her a ring for Christmas?"

"I'm not admitting anything."

"Cheapskate," Emma muttered, then helped Loretta slide Candy into her stroller. "Whose kid is he, anyway, Loretta? He certainly doesn't get that cheap streak from me or Clyde. I know his father isn't cheap. And you'd spend money as fast as the corporation could make it if the IRS would let you. So how the hell'd he get so cheap?"

Gabe listened to his grandmother sputter as she and his mother strolled Candy away, then he turned to Kassandra. "Sorry about that," he said before he realized he was being inordinately nice to her again. Or, at least, nice to her when he didn't have to be.

"I was just about to apologize to you," Kassandra said, standing beside him as the two of them watched his mother and grandmother disappear into another department store with Kassandra's baby. "I should have thought of a ring. I don't know how or why I didn't."

"Well, let's go," Gabe said, clutching her elbow to steer her in the direction of Arnold Feinburg's store. "We've got to get you a ring."

"But we..."

"I already insinuated to my grandmother that I was giving you a ring for Christmas. Now I not only have to buy one or look like a lying idiot, but I also have to get you some other gifts. You might as well pick out things you'll like."

Kassandra stopped and stared at him. "You want me to *keep* these things?"

"Well, I'm certainly not going to keep a bunch of sweaters and perfume."

"Don't you have other women you could give them to?" Kassandra asked, sounding appalled that he expected her to keep personal items from him, and Gabe felt his composure break.

"As a matter of fact, I do," he said, holding a tight rein on his anger, because he didn't understand it. Why the hell did it matter so much that she didn't want to keep his gifts? "So come help me pick out some *expensive* perfumes, a pair of diamond earrings, and...let's see...something sheer and red and really disgusting. Something that will be more of a gift for me than the woman I choose to give it to."

Gabe had the satisfaction of watching her face turn as red as the nightie he wanted her to pick out for him. "I'm not opening some vulgar piece of froth in front of your parents and grandmother," she retorted.

He smiled. "You don't have to. I'll be hiding that one in my suitcase."

Chapter Seven

For one of his bimbos, no doubt, Kassandra thought angrily as she dressed herself and Candy for breakfast the following Tuesday. Days had gone by. *Days.* And she still couldn't get the image of the red thing out of her head. Oh, it made her so mad that he'd used her. They both knew most of the women he dated were head and shoulders taller than she was, yet he'd stood in front of her and held that sheer piece of red fluff up against her as if gauging it to see how it would fit. He hadn't merely embarrassed her, he'd drawn a crowd.

It was no wonder she disliked him, Kassandra thought, then tickled Candy's belly because she realized she hadn't been very attentive these past few days. Though it hadn't mattered; the way Gabe's parents and grandmother had taken to Candy she was becoming a spoiled, pampered child.

Just like Gabe....

Kassandra squelched that thought before it could fully form. She wasn't going to think about him anymore.

Thinking about him and that red thing too damned much was the reason she wasn't paying enough attention to Candy. Her appetite was diminishing. She'd hardly watched any of the movies they'd gone to see.

That's enough, she told herself firmly, and this time she meant it. She'd never gotten this fanatic about anybody before, and if she didn't soon let it go she'd have to consider that Gabe embarrassing her at the department store wasn't the only reason he was always on her mind—that there were other things like attraction and interest and maybe even jealousy involved with why he kept roaming through her thoughts. And those "other things" didn't exist. Couldn't exist. Not only would she and Gabe officially be uncoupled the second they stepped on his private plane to Pennsylvania, but they were opposites. Two people who couldn't even live in the same building without fighting. Those other things couldn't exist!

"Ready for breakfast?" Emma asked as she opened Kassandra's bedroom door and let herself in.

"I think we're as ready as we'll ever be."

"Oh, she looks just darling today."

Kassandra laughed. "You say that every day."

"Well, she does."

"Emma, she's wearing an oversized sweatshirt and plain old blue jeans."

"Hey, don't let those fashion designers hear you say that," Emma cautioned, lifting Candy from the bed. "Besides, considering what I paid for those jeans, there'd better not be anything plain about them."

Kassandra bit her lip. "Actually, Emma, I'd like to talk to you about that."

"About what?" Emma asked innocently.

"About all the money you and Loretta are spending on Candy," Kassandra said quietly. "I mean, I know it's fun to splurge on a baby. They make the most terrific things for kids and it's tempting to buy everything you see, but I think the two of you have passed pampering and are teetering toward spoiling."

"Get used to it," Emma ordered casually. "You certainly don't think Loretta and I are going to grow tired of this. This kid's going to be in our lives for a long time, but it actually goes by so fast you think it's a short time." She caught Kassandra's gaze. "Spoiling children is half the fun of having them."

Kassandra was just on the verge of trying one more tactic, when she remembered that she and Candy had only two weeks and two days more in this house. Pushing Emma to stop buying Candy things wasn't merely a moot point, it also might make Emma suspicious.

She smiled. "You can't say I didn't try."

"Oh, hell, honey, I can say anything I want," Emma said with a cackle as Kassandra opened the door for her. "I'm damned near eighty and close to dying. I haven't got anything to lose anymore." In the hall, she paused and caught Kassandra's gaze again. "You'd be very wise to remember that," she added, then started down the hall toward the steps.

Confused by Emma's statement, Kassandra didn't immediately follow her. One didn't have to be intuitive to know Emma was making a point in that warning. In fact, when Kassandra really thought about their entire conversation this morning, she realized that though they might have been talking about spoiling Candy, there was a clear undercurrent of something else.... Or, Kassandra deduced suddenly, Emma could have been attempting to get Kassandra to slip the fact that Candy wasn't going to be around long enough to spoil.

Kassandra drew a sharp breath. Emma knew they weren't really engaged! Or at least suspected.

Kassandra watched Loretta meet Emma in the hallway and take Candy from her so Emma could walk down the stairs. Relieved, and also free now, Kassandra turned and started back down the hall. This wasn't something she could handle alone. She had to talk with Gabe.

She found his room easily and knocked twice. But fearing that someone would catch her in the hallway outside Gabe's room, Kassandra opened the door and slipped inside.

"Gabe?" she called out tentatively as she glanced around the bedroom.

"Gabe?" she said again, tiptoeing toward the bed. He didn't answer, but, mesmerized by the decor around her, Kassandra forgot she was supposed to be listening for him.

His bed was a simple four-poster double bed, with a bedspread in a pattern composed of dark-colored swirls. The curtains on the windows matched the spread. A huge multicolored braided oval rug covered most of the shiny hardwood floor. Kassandra took all that in with one sweeping glance. What caught her attention were the trophies and paraphernalia in a glass-doored bookcase that spanned an entire wall.

She looked around to see if Gabe was anywhere in sight, even tiptoed to the bathroom to make sure he wasn't hiding behind the door, then snuck back to the bookcase and opened the doors. There were a few Little League trophies, but there were more medals and trophies for track, and more plaques and memorabilia from high school and college football.

"I was being scouted by the pros, but my grandfather died during my senior year in college. To say Emma took it hard would be an understatement. She fell apart. So instead of joining the pros, I joined the family business."

Kassandra clutched her chest and spun around. "Geez, Gabe, are you trying to give me a heart attack?"

"I figured you must be curious to be sneaking around. So I thought I'd fill you in."

"I'm not curious . . . I mean, I wasn't curious," Kassandra admitted, though she was certainly curious now. Not only was she beginning to see that his spoiling and pampering was a double-edged sword, but now she realized he was so dedicated to his family that he'd given up a great deal for them. "That isn't why I came in here. I came in here looking for you."

Gabe smiled, his brown eyes glittering with possibilities. "Now, that's interesting."

"Yeah, it's terrifically interesting. I think Emma's on to us."

"No she's not or she wouldn't have bought Calvin Klein jeans for Candy."

"It was talking about those very Calvin Kleins that made me see she's suspicious."

Gabe frowned. "What did she say?"

"It wasn't what she said, it was how she sort of drew me in. Or tried to get me to make a slip in our conversation."

"Sounds like Emma's modus operandi, all right."

"What do you think we should do?"

He thought for a minute, then he grinned devilishly. "I have the perfect foil for her. I'll ask my parents to allow us to announce our engagement officially at their annual Christmas party."

"They have an annual Christmas party?"

"Only two hundred of their closest friends."

"Sounds cozy."

"Actually, it is," Gabe said, then meandered over to the trophy case. He picked up an old, worn football and caressed it. "I'll explain to my parents that our little discussion about the rings in the mall the other day spoiled my surprise. So I had to tell you that I was planning to give you the ring at the Christmas party, and we decided that we'd make an official announcement . . . or some such thing."

"We never did pick out a ring last week."

"I know. But it doesn't matter. We knew we'd have to get one, anyway. And when we do, Emma won't be a problem anymore. Once she sees you wearing a huge diamond there's no way she'd ever think this engagement wasn't for real."

Kassandra's eyes widened. They both knew they had to get a ring, but up until this minute Kassandra had never thought about the expense. The minute he said *huge*, however, her heart stopped.

"Gabe, maybe we should be thinking more in terms of pretty, rather than huge."

"I like huge. Grandma will like huge. You heard how she always calls me a cheapskate. This ought to nip that in the bud, too."

"And what will you do with the *huge* diamond once we get back to Pennsylvania?" she said, seeking to make her point without being obvious.

He smiled. "That's no problem," Gabe said casually. After one last look at the football, he set it back in the bookcase, then secured the latch. Resting his arm along her shoulders, he turned her in the direction of his bedroom door. "We'll get a ring from Arnold Feinburg, and then we'll drop it off again on our way to the airport the day after New Year's." He shrugged carelessly. "That's what friends are for."

Any sympathy that might have been forming for him fizzled instantly. "Anybody ever tell you you're one lucky guy?"

"I'm not lucky. I'm well connected. There's a big difference."

"And that difference is?"

"Lucky people never get into trouble. Or, if they do, someone else rescues them. I get into trouble all the time, but I have to get myself out. Luckily—" he smiled cockily at her "—I'm well connected enough to be able to do it."

Not wanting to touch that statement with a ten-foot pole, Kassandra walked away from him, keeping her pace quick so she stayed ahead of him and didn't have to talk to him anymore. When she reached the bottom of the steps, however, she waited for him so they could enter the dining room together.

"All right," he said, sounding like a director for a movie. "Big smiles, everyone. Let's look like we're enjoying this."

Kassandra shook her head at his silliness, but when they stepped over the threshold into his parents' formal dining room, she was smiling broadly.

"The baby's already had her oatmeal," Loretta announced.

Glancing at the smeared bib that protected Candy's sweatshirt and jeans, Kassandra said, "I see."

"So where were the two of you?" Emma asked loudly.

Gabe said "Dressing" at the very second that Kassandra said "Talking," and Kassandra blushed furiously. Fortunately, getting embarrassed over that kind of mistake might have made them look like liars, but they looked like liars trying to steal a few private minutes, which engaged people would do.

"Never mind," Loretta briskly said, then changed the subject as she turned to Kassandra. "Emma, Sam and I are going to start decorating this morning, Kassandra. We'd love to have Candy help us."

"*I'd* love to help you!" Kassandra said, unexpectedly realizing that this was the first Christmas holiday she'd be able to enjoy in almost four years. She didn't have a second job to go to over her holiday vacation. She didn't have tips to be super polite for, or even other people's Christmas parties to help cater. She was a free woman for the first time since she started college.

"You can't, sweetheart," Gabe said, then rested his arm across her shoulders. Once again, it was starting to feel comfortable there. "Don't you remember that little errand you and I have to run this morning?"

"What errand?" Emma demanded. "What could be more important than decorating with your family?"

"Kassandra and I are going shopping for her ring this morning."

Loretta gasped with appreciation and her eyes got misty, but Emma shook her head and said, "It's about time."

"Mother," Sam cautioned. "Don't you think you're being a little pushy here?"

"A person's not really engaged until she has a ring," she groused.

"Exactly what we thought," Gabe said, pulling Kassandra a little closer.

She could smell his cologne and suddenly felt disoriented. Not only was she pressed up against him and sniffing his wonderful cologne, but she liked it. Remembering why she wasn't supposed to like it became difficult, then hazy, and eventually she stopped trying.

"Not only are we choosing a ring today, but we'd like your permission to announce our engagement at your Christmas party on Saturday."

"Saturday?" Kassandra gasped, looking at Gabe. "You never told me the Christmas party was Saturday."

But no one seemed to hear her. Sam and Loretta rose from their seats. Loretta ran over and hugged Gabe and then Kassandra.

Sam shook Gabe's hand. "This is wonderful," he said.

"Perfect," Loretta said, her eyes filled with tears. "I have a million things to do."

"Why?" Gabe asked. "We're only announcing our engagement. That shouldn't make any extra work for you."

"Oh, my goodness, yes," Loretta said. "First, the dress I bought is good enough for a Christmas party, but not to announce my only son's engagement. Second, there are probably fifty more people I should invite to hear this news. Third, your father and I will need to buy you some sort of engagement gift...."

"No, mother, don't go overboard," Gabe began, but Kassandra, seeing the shrewd look on Emma's face, kicked him in the shin.

"Gabe, don't ruin your mother's fun," Kassandra said, then turned and kissed his cheek. "I'd love to come with you when you choose your dress, Loretta," she added happily. "To tell you the truth, I should get something new, too."

"All right," Loretta said, looking perfectly within her element as a planner. "You and Gabe pick out the ring today, then you and I will hit the good stores tomorrow."

"I'll be hitting those same stores with you," Emma said, rising from her chair. "I could use a new dress, too. I think I'll buy something red-sequined and backless."

"I think you'll scare the neighbors if you do," Sam said, directing her to sit again. "None of us is going anywhere until I've had breakfast."

Chapter Eight

Gabe picked out a ring that was more gaudy than romantic. At least four carats, it gleamed atop a solid gold setting. When Kassandra put it on her finger, her hand felt as if it weighed ten pounds. The minute Arnold Feinburg was out of earshot, she ripped it off and handed it to Gabe. "I would never wear this."

"Well, this is exactly what I'd buy a woman I truly loved."

"That's why you'll never pull off this charade," Kassandra said, then motioned for Arnold to get out a tray of less expensive rings. These had diamonds that sparkled and winked, but didn't threaten anyone with blindness. Some were surrounded by baguettes. Some had been crafted into romantic settings of antique gold. Some were heart-shaped. "You have poor taste, and your grandmother would never believe I'd choose that ring," she said, pointing at the monstrosity that Gabe held. "But any one of these your grandmother will fall in love with."

"She's right, Gabe," Arnold said, smiling knowingly at Gabe. "And your grandmother's the one you want to please here, if you stop to think about it."

"All right," Gabe grudgingly agreed. "Which one would you choose?"

"That one," Kassandra answered without hesitation, reaching for a one-carat marquise flanked by four baguettes, two on each side.

"Excellent choice," Arnold agreed. "That shape will look wonderful on your hand."

Gabe took the ring from Kassandra to examine it. "Not bad," he admitted reluctantly. "It's got enough stones that my grandmother won't think I'm cheap, and it is sort of pretty in a fancy kind of way."

"It's gorgeous," Kassandra corrected him. "Emma will love it."

"You're sure?" Gabe asked, carefully studying the ring.

"Slip it on her finger, Gabe," Arnold said. "You're going to love it once you see how it looks on."

Gabe did exactly as he was told. Without any thought, he took Kassandra's fingers in his hand, separated her ring finger and poised the ring to slide it on, but the strangest thing happened. He picked that exact second to look into her eyes and saw she was watching him. Not merely looking at him, but studying him as if she'd only recently discovered something about him and it had changed her opinion of him.

He hadn't expected her to be impressed by the discovery that his parents had saved every piece of sports memorabilia since he was old enough to wear a hat. If anything, he was just about positive that would only make her consider him more spoiled.

But this look wasn't a look that said she thought he was spoiled. This look was dark and dangerous. This was a look that said she was seeing him—*him*—not the person he pretended to be, not the person everybody thought he was, but

him, for perhaps the first time. Probably because he'd ca-
pitulated so easily on the ring choice. Something he'd never
done with her before.

It wasn't a good breakthrough. Not if they planned on
playing out this charade for the entire holiday. And Gabe
had every intention of doing that. Not merely because he
wanted to fulfill his grandmother's wish, but also because
he didn't want his family to catch him in a lie. Particularly
not now that he'd gone so far to make this lie stick.

He glanced away, down at her hand, and slid the ring over
Kassandra's knuckle. It fit as if it were made for her, and,
as Arnold had said, it looked remarkably beautiful on her
long, tapered finger.

"It's wonderful," he admitted quietly, suddenly realizing that her hands were soft and warm and she hadn't
jumped away from him...or yelled at him in the past hour.
Combining those things with the look she was giving him,
Gabe abruptly felt nervous. Antsy. Like he had to get the
hell out of here. "We'll take this one, Arnold," Gabe said,
and rose from his seat. "One more favor?"

Arnold smiled his jeweler smile. "Anything."

"Could you wrap it?"

"Sure."

"I'll wrap it!" Kassandra said as if she were shocked by
Gabe's inconsiderateness.

"Emma will be able to tell if it hasn't been wrapped here."

"She will," Arnold assured her. "Just let me take care of
everything."

"We'll have the ring back January 2—you know the situation. We'll drop it off on our way to the airport."

"Sure. Fine. Whenever," Arnold said, ushering them to
the door. "I'm in no hurry."

They left the jewelry store, and out of habit Gabe glanced
at his watch. It was only a quarter after ten. He sighed. "We
have some time to kill." And the last person he wanted to
spend it with was her. Not because he didn't like her, but

because he *did* like her—or at least he was starting to. And that would not only make the charade uncomfortable, it wouldn't make for a nice, clean break in Pennsylvania.

Indifferent, Kassandra looked around. "Have you done your shopping for your parents and grandmother yet?"

He shook his head. "No. I usually wait until Christmas Eve."

"Well, this year we'll shake things up a bit," Kassandra said, hooking her hand in his elbow. "We'll buy your gifts this morning. I'll help you."

Suddenly the nervous, antsy feeling was back again. Gabe was absolutely positive he didn't want to do this. Not that he didn't appreciate help with his shopping; he certainly did. But he just felt odd about *her* helping him. And he knew why he felt nervous. Shopping for her fake Christmas presents the other day had gotten too personal, too intimate. Showing her his taste was like giving her a peek into his private life. Finding out what gifts she thought were attractive or useful was like getting a peek into hers. Without trying, they had begun to get to know each other. And that wasn't good. Not at all. Not even a little bit.

But there was nothing else to do, and they had at least three hours to kill. Besides, he had *let* it get too personal the other day. That's why he'd forced her to stay with him while he picked out the sexy red thing. It was the best way to remind both of them they were from two different worlds.

He could do that today, if things got too cozy. In fact, he decided to look at this as a happy accident that he had someone to help him select gifts this year and treat her as something like an employee. Then there would be no danger that he'd appreciate what she was doing for him.

It didn't work.

Two hours later, laden with armloads of presents he knew his family would adore, Gabe was being led into a restaurant by a chatting fake fiancée. They'd spent the morning happily, almost joyfully, choosing gifts, and things had spiraled out of hand. Not only was she now catching almost every joke he made, but Gabe didn't feel the usual knot of tension he felt at the back of his neck every time she was within three feet of him....

Damn it! They were getting along!

They *had to* get along in front of his family, but he didn't want them getting cozy otherwise. He didn't want any complications, and becoming too friendly with a happily-ever-after woman like Kassandra was certainly a complication.

And she was a happily-ever-after woman if ever he'd seen a happily-ever-after woman. Anybody who wouldn't marry the father of her child because she wasn't quite sure she loved him was definitely looking for happily-ever-after. If all this got too snug, too comfortable, too *friendly* down here, then they wouldn't be parting company at the airport.

Which wasn't what he wanted. When they went home he wanted to be sure they went back to living their separate, albeit antagonistic, lives. And the best way to ensure that would be to keep their antagonism alive and well so she didn't get any ideas.

A waiter came, took their orders and disappeared. Kassandra smiled at Gabe, confirming all his prior suspicions.

"So, you rejected an offer from the pros, huh?"

"I'm sorry, Kassandra," he said, as nice as he could be considering that his real goal was to reestablish their emotional distance. Maybe even revive their animosity. "But that's none of your business."

"Oh, I'm sorry. I didn't mean to pry."

"Just like this morning, you didn't mean to be snooping through my room."

"I wasn't snooping, I . . ."

"You were looking through my things—had opened a door to get into a cabinet. I'd call that snooping."

She stiffened. "I'm sorry," she apologized sincerely, and as if by magic she turned back into the restrained woman who lived across the hall from him in Pennsylvania, the one he didn't like. "I don't typically do things like that. My only excuse is that I was curious because I still need more information about you. Your grandmother is very shrewd. If there's a mistake to be made, I don't want to be the one to make it."

"Well, let me put your mind at rest," Gabe said, leveling what he knew would be the final blow to ensure the woman he didn't like stayed with him, particularly when they were alone. "If either one or both of us makes a slip that ruins the charade, you'll still get paid."

She sucked in air between her teeth, but Gabe noticed she didn't offer to refuse his money if she made the mistake. . . .

They might be in Georgia, but as far as their relationship was concerned, they were back on their home turf.

Gabe and Kassandra stepped into the foyer and saw Sam and Loretta lacing the cherry-wood banister with garland while Emma, standing at the bottom with Candy, issued orders. Because they hadn't been expecting to see anyone the second they walked through the front door, both Gabe and Kassandra scrambled to stand closer. When they did, Kassandra accidentally stepped on Gabe's foot, and there was a definite lack of sincerity in her voice when she apologized.

"You two look like you had a productive day," Loretta said in a singsong voice as she looped garlands of silver-and-red tinsel around the banister, then handed it to Sam.

"Oh, we did," Gabe said happily. "Kassandra chose some wonderful gifts. This is the first Christmas I won't have to save receipts."

"You've never had to save receipts before," Emma grumbled, carrying Candy to a plate of cookies that sat on a small table along a foyer wall. "McDonald's doesn't allow you to return gift certificates for French fries and soft drinks.''

''Very funny,'' Gabe groused lovingly.

''I thought it was,'' Emma agreed, then turned toward the stairway. ''I still say we should have added a strip of green tinsel, too.''

''It's too much.''

''Nothing's ever too much for Christmas.''

''I agree,'' Kassandra said, inhaling deeply to catch the scent of pine and fresh-baked cookies. The world beyond the door might be a comfortable fifty degrees, but inside it felt and smelled like a snowy, wintery Christmas.

''See, I told you this woman would be good for Gabe,'' Emma said proudly. She turned to Kassandra. ''I hope you didn't shop yourself out today. We still have to go for new dresses tomorrow.''

For a second Kassandra felt disoriented, because not only had she forgotten all about that trip, but Emma was acting as if nothing was wrong, completely opposite from the way she'd acted in Kassandra's room that morning. Still, remembering that that was the precise effect Gabe had hoped to gain with the ring and the official announcement, Kassandra smiled. ''I never tire of shopping.''

''That's my girl,'' Loretta said, then brushed off her hands as she admired her handiwork. ''I like it.''

''It passes,'' Emma grumbled.

Kassandra laughed. ''Well, I'm going to take Candy up to bed for her nap now, if no one minds.''

''She just got a cookie, dear,'' Emma said. ''Why don't you go on up and I'll bring her when she's finished?''

''Okay,'' Kassandra said, and started up the stairway. She sensed more than saw that Gabe was following her, but didn't pay much attention since he had to take his packages to his room. When he stopped outside her door, though, she narrowed her eyes at him.

''What do you want?''

"I want to talk to you. Inside," he said, nudging his head toward her bedroom door.

She sighed. "Is this important?"

"Very."

With another labored sigh, she pushed open the door and walked inside. Gabe followed, threw his packages on her bed and pulled out his wallet. "How much is this dress of yours going to cost?"

"I have no idea."

"Give me a rough estimate so I can give you some money and be on my way."

She straightened her spine and shot him a look she knew would drop a panther at forty yards. "I don't want your money."

"Oh, come on, take the damned money."

"I said, I don't want your money."

"Look," he said, kinder now. "I know you can't afford to buy a dress, and you wouldn't be buying a dress if you weren't here, so it's my responsibility to pay for it."

"I plan on buying something I can wear again next Christmas, so you needn't concern yourself," Kassandra said, and avoided looking at his face because she felt like he was starting to pity her, and that would make her madder than she already was.

He sighed. She continued to ignore him by hanging up her coat and slipping out of her shoes.

"Kassie, the stores my mother and grandmother shop at are *very* expensive."

"Then we'll just have to go to other stores."

"Even other stores are going to be more than you can afford."

"Not if I bargain shop."

"You are not bargain shopping in front of my mother and grandmother!" Gabe exploded, as angry as she was now.

"That, Mr. Cayne, to coin your phrase, is none of your business."

"It is *completely* my business!" he thundered, ripping several hundred dollar bills from his wallet and throwing them on her dresser. "You use that!"

"Don't you ever throw money on my dresser again!" she returned, every bit as angry. "If you don't get it off in three seconds I am out of here.... And I mean out of here, as in flying back to Pennsylvania."

Gabe stared at Kassandra.

Kassandra stared at Gabe.

For a full thirty seconds, neither said anything, then, with a curse, he grabbed the money from her dresser. Almost simultaneously, there was a knock at Kassandra's door.

"Come in," Kassandra barked, instantly regretting that she spoke before she thought.

Emma hesitated on the threshold, holding cookie-faced Candy. "I hope I'm not interrupting anything," she said uncertainly, and from the tone of her voice Kassandra could tell she knew very well that she was interrupting something, that she might have even chosen that precise second to knock in order to interrupt their argument.

"No, you're not interrupting anything," Kassandra said, recovering quickly. "Gabe and I are just having a little fight over money. He wants to pay for my party dress. I want to keep my independence."

"Well, I know that," Emma said briskly, bustling into the room with Candy. "For Pete's sake, I could hear you in the hall."

As she said the last, Gabe and Kassandra glanced at each other. If Emma had heard that much, neither could be sure she hadn't heard even more of the conversation. With an apologetic smile, Gabe reached for Kassandra. "I'm very sorry," he said, and though Kassandra knew he was only acting for Emma's benefit, she wished he really was sorry. Not sorry for arguing about the dress, but for treating her so coldly in the restaurant. Just when she was starting to think he wasn't quite as bad as his reputation warranted, he'd turned into a jerk again.

Which probably was for the best, she thought, realizing that he was going to kiss her. She didn't want to think of him as nice. Yet she was beginning to see his good side, starting to like him, and to think he might be liking her, too. But from the things he said to her in the restaurant, obviously he wasn't. And she would do well to remember that.

Still, when his lips met hers, all her good logic flew out the window. He might not be falling for her, but she was falling for him. Fast and hard. Ridiculously fast and hard. That's why his telling her his life was none of her business had hurt her so much and why the light brush of his lips across hers right now felt like pure heaven.

"There now, isn't that better?" Emma said, intruding much to Kassandra's regret and relief. This charade was turning on her, and unless she got hold of herself right now, she wouldn't ever get hold of herself.

When she pulled away from Gabe, she saw that his eyes were transfixed on her face, and she reminded herself that unlike her, he hadn't been feeling the stirring of his soul—a little passion maybe, but nothing deeper, nothing more serious. If he was staring at her lovingly, it was an act for his grandmother's benefit.

"You better get this kid washed off and in her crib for a nap," Emma advised, shuffling toward the door, but as she passed Kassandra she said in a stage whisper, "Independence is fine, but if I were you I'd take his money, dear." Then she shuffled out the door, closing it behind her.

"See, even my grandmother thinks you should take this money," Gabe said sincerely, still gazing into her eyes.

For a few seconds, she stood enthralled, almost mesmerized, then his words from the restaurant came back to haunt her and she abruptly pulled away. "No, thanks."

He pulled away, too. "Fine," he said, and started for the door.

She stopped him. "Gabe, you don't have to worry. I may bargain shop, but I have good taste. I won't embarrass you."

For some reason or another that seemed to irritate him. He pushed out of the door and slammed it behind him.

Chapter Nine

Sitting on wing chairs outside the dressing room of an exclusive Atlanta dress shop, Emma and Kassandra waited as Loretta tried on her fifth dress.

Without warning, Emma turned to Kassandra. "I couldn't help but notice how angry you and Gabe get when you fight."

Brought out of her thoughts, Kassandra glanced at Gabe's grandmother and said, "Excuse me?"

"I said I couldn't help but notice how angry you and Gabe get when you fight."

Not quite sure how much of the argument from the day before Emma had heard, and trying to downplay the significance of the disagreement the easiest way possible, Kassandra smiled and said, "Emma, that's just chemistry."

Emma gaped at her. "Chemistry?"

"Sure, Gabe and I are different, yet we're very attracted to each other," Kassandra said casually. "So we fight all the time. Chemistry... or fighting... is sometimes fate's only way of bringing different kinds of people together...."

As she said the last, Kassandra got a peculiar sensation in the pit of her stomach. What she'd just said was true. Even though she'd been able to live in his exclusive apartment building by pooling her money with two friends, Kassandra never would have met Gabriel Cayne if he hadn't awakened Candy.

Emma frowned. "You met each other because you were fighting?"

"Noise from one of his parties awakened Candy," Kassandra said, confused because, once again, the truth was turning out to be very believable. "So I went across the hall to his apartment to get him to tone it down."

"And he saw how beautiful you were and invited you in," Emma speculated curiously.

"Not exactly."

Loretta picked that precise second to come waltzing out of the dressing room, modeling her new pink gown. "It makes your butt look big, dear," Emma said, and Loretta went scampering into the dressing room as if her shoes were on fire. "Try that pretty pearl gray thing," Emma called after her.

The minute Loretta was out of earshot, Emma turned to Kassandra again. "Then what *exactly* happened?" she asked seriously.

"One day he helped me when my grocery bag broke, and we both realized the other wasn't quite so bad. Then he asked me to go somewhere with him, and I did, and now here we are," Kassandra said, mesmerized by the truth, because the truth wasn't merely believable, it was a good, almost romantic story—at least in its abbreviated, generic form. "I don't remember specific details," she added, to ensure the story stayed abbreviated and generic because she recognized that the unabridged version wasn't quite as charming. "But I do know that deep down inside Gabe and I love each other. And though we argue about stupid, inconsequential things like money, we agree on all the important stuff."

"Like what?"

Kassandra glanced at Emma again. "Meaning what things do we agree on?"

Emma nodded. "Yeah. What are the things you agree on?"

"Well," Kassandra said, then she swallowed, wondering if she wasn't falling into another of Emma's traps. She'd been so caught up in the fact that so much of their story did seem believable and almost romantic, she didn't pay enough attention to the direction in which Emma was steering the conversation. Trying to get things back to their abbreviated, generic state, she said, "You know. Things. The important things."

"Like whether or not you'll finish school?" Emma asked.

"Yes. Gabe and I both agree I should finish school," Kassandra happily said, because that was the truth. She and Gabe did agree that she should finish school. Admitting to that wasn't risky or wrong.

"And, of course, since you're telling me you think you agree on the important things, that means you and Gabe also agree on how you'll raise Candy."

Another truth. She and Gabe did agree on how Candy should be raised. By Kassandra. No problem with agreeing with that. She smiled. "Yes, in fact, Gabe and I do agree on how Candy will be raised."

"That's wonderful, dear," Emma said noncommittally, turning her attention to the dressing room door again. "You know, in all honesty, we were struck dumb when Gabe brought you and Candy to meet us. First, because you were so different from any of the other women he's dated. Second, because Gabe's never had an interest in children before. It absolutely amazed Loretta and me that he volunteered to baby-sit this morning, but now I'm really glad he did."

Emma paused as if making sure she had Kassandra's complete attention before she said, "You can tell a lot about a relationship from the way a man interacts with a woman's baby. Especially when he baby-sits." Then she rose as Loretta came out of the dressing room. "Now, that's more like it! Don't you think so, Kassandra?"

Kassandra looked perfectly calm when she nodded, but inside her stomach had begun to quiver. This time she knew she wasn't imagining things. As sure as Kassandra was sitting on a blue wing chair, she knew Emma still suspected something was wrong with her relationship with Gabe. In essence, Emma had just said that Kassandra and Gabe might be able to cover all their bases, but Emma was counting on Gabe to slip up with Candy.

If Gabe didn't take good care of Candy this morning, this charade was as good as over.

Gabe stared at the rectangular strip of plastic and cotton and turned it several possible ways before finally sliding it beneath Candy's bottom. He'd watched Honey, the downstairs maid, diaper Candy through the two false alarms they'd had right after Kassandra left this morning. Now that a real emergency had arisen, he was too embarrassed to call her again.

Besides, he wasn't quite sure she'd answer if he called.

But it didn't matter. He had this diaper thing under control.

"Don't I, Candy?" he crooned, and she grinned at him.

"This isn't so hard," he said, yanking on a plastic strip to place it across the front of the diaper, but for some reason or another the sticky side was on the outside, away from the diaper. After a few seconds of staring, the engineering properties of the garment dawned on him and he folded the top down, to cuff it, which put the sticky side exactly where he wanted it. After fastening both sides, he lifted Candy in the air and eyed his handiwork. The plastic was inside to protect her clothing from the inevitable. The soft cotton was outside, looking clean and white.

"There, now," he said, laying Candy down again. "See, I'm not a complete idiot about this stuff. I don't know what the big deal is." He tickled her belly once for good measure, then he slid on her jeans, put on her socks and shoes, and carried her downstairs.

Once in the family room, he took a seat on the comfortable floral sofa, organized Candy on his lap and reached for a contract from his open briefcase, which was on the square coffee table. The very second he had the contract arranged at eye level, Candy began patting it with a slobber-covered fist.

"Oh, no," Gabe said, snatching it out of her way with one hand as he steadied her roly-poly body with his other hand. "You can't ruin this. It was drawn up by the other side's attorney," he explained rationally. "It's already signed by the guy who runs the company I'm negotiating with. So, if I like it and I sign it, then they can't take any of these provisions back. They're locked in."

Candy wiped her nose with her hand, then shook her head furiously.

"I know what you're thinking," Gabe said. "If the other side's already signed it then it's not good for me." He set the contract on the sofa, away from Candy, but close enough that he could still see it. "You're right. It's wishful thinking to believe it's going to be good as is. But I still have to read it."

She grinned at him, then bent forward and grabbed for the bright white document.

He snatched the contract out of her reach and tossed it on the table. "This isn't going to work. I have to fax this back to my office this afternoon. And," he said, glancing around, "I have to keep you out of trouble."

Candy gurgled at him.

Gabe rubbed his hand over his mouth. He couldn't hold his contract in front of her, because she wanted to play with it, but unless he held his contract about where she was sitting on his lap, then he couldn't see it to read it.

Unless...

By the time Emma, Loretta and Kassandra arrived home from shopping, Kassandra was as nervous as a woman could get. Not only had Emma's comments caused her to truly worry about how well Gabe could take care of Candy, but she reasoned that once Emma had confirmation this engagement was bogus, she would undoubtedly confront them.

Recognizing this, Kassandra was ready to talk Gabe into confessing before Emma challenged them. But in order for Kassandra to convince Gabe to confess, she had to get an opportunity to talk to him—alone. And that wasn't going to be easy. Not with the way Emma had dogged her all morning.

As they opened the front door, Kassandra grabbed the packages from Emma's hands. "I'll take these upstairs for you, and you can make arrangements with Honey to get a cup of tea."

"Why, thank you, dear," Emma said sweetly. "But I think I'd better follow you up to show you which room to put my packages in."

Kassandra smiled as best she could. "Oh, okay. I never thought of that." So much for keeping Emma downstairs. On the bright side, since they'd already be in Emma's room, Kassandra decided she might be able to talk Emma into a nap once her packages were deposited. Then Kassandra could warn Gabe that his grandmother was looking to see how well he'd cared for Candy. A long nap would give Kassandra time to teach him some basic baby-sitting skills, and also to clean up any disasters that might have occurred in her absence.

Smiling, Kassandra put Emma's packages on her bed and suggested a nap, but Emma wouldn't have any of it. Instead, she followed Kassandra into the hall and toward the room Kassandra shared with Candy, using the excuse that once Kassandra's purchases were taken care of they'd both have tea.

Trying to be inconspicuous, Kassandra cracked the thick door an inch and peeked in, hoping that if Gabe was in her room with Candy, Kassandra could get a preview of whether or not it was safe for his grandmother to see the scene. But Gabe wasn't in her room.

Puzzled, she stowed her bundles, then followed Emma as she returned to the main floor of the house.

"I'll bet they're in the family room," Emma said in a voice that sounded reassuring.

Kassandra nodded and led the way down the hall to the comfortable, spacious room in which the Cayne family played board games and cards and sometimes watched television. She stepped over the threshold, and when she saw the scene in front of her, she didn't know whether to laugh or cry. Gabe lay on the sofa, reading a contract, with Candy imprisoned by his feet. But the baby didn't seem to mind. She patted his ankles, teethed on his sock-covered toes and nuzzled the bottoms of his feet.

Kassandra held her breath. This was it. Emma would surely realize Gabe had never cared for a baby before, and she'd confront them.

Ready to take her medicine, Kassandra faced Emma, but Emma didn't say anything. She only gaped at the scene before her.

Obviously seeing the shocked expressions on both Kassandra's and Emma's faces, Gabe said, "My feet were the only things she couldn't hurt herself on if she bumped them, and the only things her slobber and biting wouldn't damage." He waved some legal papers at them. "This arrived by fax about a minute after you left. I have to fax my comments back by four. I didn't have a choice.''

''I see,'' Emma said, apparently thinking Gabe's baby-sitting technique appropriate given the circumstances. Oddly subdued, she reached out and removed Candy from the sofa, but when she did her face scrunched up in confusion. ''What's this?'' she asked, then pulled the elastic band of Candy's jeans away to examine her diaper.

She gasped, looked at Gabe, then looked at Kassandra. ''Her diaper is on inside out!''

''It is?'' Kassandra asked, dismayed.

''It is?'' Gabe asked, confused.

''It is,'' Emma said, handing Candy to Kassandra. ''I'm suddenly feeling very tired. If you'll excuse me, I think I will take that nap.''

Shoulders slumped, Emma trudged toward the open doorway, and a wave of empathy washed over Kassandra. She knew exactly how disappointed Emma felt, and knowing that made Kassandra feel guilty and loathsome both at the same time. Emma walked out of the room and down the long, lonely corridor to the foyer and the stairway, and Kassandra felt about two inches tall. She should have known this scheme wouldn't work. But more than that, Gabe should have known.

''We should be ashamed of ourselves for trying to deceive your grandmother,'' Kassandra muttered as she began walking out of the family room. ''I'm going to tell her the truth and apologize to her.''

''Whoa! Whoa! Wait a minute,'' Gabe said, jumping from the sofa and scrambling after her. He caught her elbow as she reached the hallway and, as if it were the most natural thing in the world, took Candy from her arms. ''What are you talking about?'' he asked as Candy wrapped her chubby little arms around his neck and cuddled up to him.

''Your grandmother,'' Kassandra said, angry now.

"What about my grandmother?" Gabe asked, stroking Candy's back as she snuggled into his neck.

Candy's behavior temporarily stole Kassandra's concern. "When was the last time *Candy* napped?" Kassandra asked, then pushed a wayward wisp of her daughter's hair from her forehead.

"I don't know," Gabe said. "I guess she didn't nap."

"Then she's going to have to nap now," Kassandra said, and began marching up the hall. "We'll put her in bed, then I think we should both go to your grandmother and tell her the truth."

"Wait. Whoa!" Gabe said, still scurrying to keep up with her. "Something happened today, and before we break down and ruin a perfectly good plan, I think you'd better explain it to me."

"She's on to us," Kassandra said, exasperated that he seemed so thickheaded.

"Shh!" Gabe hissed. "Not so loud. Better yet, save it until we get behind closed doors."

Agitated, Kassandra unhappily did as she was asked, but the second the door closed behind them, she turned on Gabe. "She heard enough yesterday to lead me into a conversation this morning to try to get me to admit something was wrong. When I didn't bite, she kept pushing, wanting me to slip something that would prove you and I haven't held an in-depth, private discussion."

Unconcerned, Gabe shrugged, then handed Candy to her mother. "None of my friends have had in-depth conversations with their wives. That's perfectly normal."

"Maybe for you," Kassandra said, stripping Candy's jeans and T-shirt away, changing her diaper and dressing her in one-piece pajamas. "But not for me, and your grandmother knows that."

"Well, damn it, why did you have to say anything?"

She whirled on him. "You sanctimonious jerk. I didn't say anything! But even if I had it was only because I was trying to get us out of trouble for the conversation Emma overheard yesterday. The one in which *you* were shouting, not me.'' Frustrated, Kassandra stopped herself, laid Candy in her crib, then combed her fingers through her hair. "Look, let's face it. We put this together too fast. We didn't have a plan. We didn't create any good stories and we got caught.''

"You *think* we got caught.''

Kassandra sighed. "Gabe, I'm smart enough to know that your grandmother's disappointed. And you want to know what's worse? She's not disappointed that you're not engaged. She's disappointed that you lied to her.''

"Exactly,'' Gabe said, and sat on the bed. His thoughts were going a hundred miles a second, but the only thing they kept coming back to was the fact that he couldn't admit defeat. All of this had started out with such wonderful purposes. He wanted his grandmother to be happy, so he created a fiancée. He didn't want to disappoint her, so he found someone to play his fiancée so he could keep the charade going. None of this came about for malicious purposes. Only good. It didn't seem fair to break it all down, and depress his grandmother to hell and back, when it had all started out as being something to make her happy.

"I can't tell her that I lied,'' Gabe said quietly. From the short contact he'd had with Emma this afternoon, Gabe couldn't really be sure if Emma knew or if Kassandra was only panicking. But as agitated and convinced as Kassandra was, Gabe knew if he said that she'd flip out on him again. "I just can't do it.''

"Gabe, she knows,'' Kassandra softly insisted. "It's not just a sense I have anymore. I can tell by her behavior. And the longer you keep this up, the more disappointed she's going to be when you tell her.''

"Not if we figure a way to patch the holes in our story.''

"We've already got a quilt and a half. I don't think any more patching will help.''

"Then we have to do something dramatic."

"Like what?"

"I don't know, something that pushes her over the top," Gabe said, springing from the bed and beginning to pace. "Something that makes her believe us."

Kassandra shook her head. "Gabe, we'd need hours of explaining. We fight, she's heard us. We don't know much about each other's lives. And you can't put on a diaper," she said, frustrated. "What could we possibly do that would make her believe we're getting married?"

Unexpectedly Gabe's face lit up. "Set a date," he said, then he grinned. "Set the Christmas date."

Understanding what he was saying, Kassandra backed away from him. "Oh, no," she said, shaking her head. "No. No. No."

"Why not?" Gabe asked ingeniously. "I have two friends. One's a minister. One's an actor. The minister could marry us, and then we could secretly have the marriage annulled. Or the actor could pretend to marry us. And on January 2, we'd get on that plane the same two people who took off from Pennsylvania in December. Not married, not anything. And no one has to be any the wiser."

"You're nuts!"

"No. Hear me out. It's really a very simple plan."

"So was the fake engagement a simple plan and look where that got us," Kassandra reminded him. "Besides, how are we going to get out of this? What are you going to tell Emma at Easter when Candy and I don't show up?"

Gabe cleared his throat. "We both know my grandmother won't be around for Easter."

Hearing the controlled quiver in Gabe's voice, Kassandra sat on the bed. Emma might be spry, but she wasn't well. She took rests in the stores in which they shopped, ate differently from the rest of the family, took naps and hardly participated during family times. Kassandra knew exactly what he was saying. She also knew how much losing his grandmother hurt him, and how much protecting her meant to him.

"Please," he said, walking to the bed and kneeling in front of her. "I'll give you anything you want. It just seems pointless to hurt her when we don't have to."

She licked her lips. "All right," she agreed quietly. "But we use the actor, not the minister, and I want you to promise that eventually you'll confess to your parents."

"Scout's honor," he agreed, relieved.

"And you have to promise me that we'll work closely on this. No more fighting. Whenever we have a problem, we discuss it and we work out a plan to solve it. Neither one of us makes up a story or makes a plan without the other."

"Agreed."

"We're going to have to act happier in front of your family."

"You've got it," he said, then he winced. "Kassie, that might be the point you have to agree on."

"I do agree with it."

"Well, when we say act happier in front of my family, that really means we have to act more like an engaged couple."

Finally understanding what he was saying, Kassandra said, "Oh."

"We're going to have to hold hands more."

She conceded that with a nod. "Okay."

"And maybe hug every once in a while."

"I can do that."

"And kiss more often—much more often than what we've been doing."

Even thinking about kissing him more often made her want to shiver, but he was right, so she agreed. "Okay. No problem."

Their gazes caught and held for about three seconds, then Gabe leaned forward and gently pressed his lips against Kassandra's. In spite of the fact that Kassandra knew he was kissing her for practice, or to prove a point, there was something about this kiss that made it real. Not because it was deep and penetrating, or even full of passion and fire, but because this kiss was soft and emotional—almost as if he were thanking her for agreeing to help him.

Slowly, reluctantly, he pulled away. "Now, explain the diaper thing to me so I don't get us in hot water again."

Swallowing, Kassandra nodded. Still tingling and caught in the gaze from his deep brown eyes, she realized the greatest danger in this charade wasn't disappointing Gabe's grandmother, but that she'd started to fall in love with him.

Chapter Ten

At dinner that night, Gabe waited for a congenial pause in the conversation, then said, "Mother, Kassandra and I were hoping you'd rethink your Christmas party this year."

Loretta looked up from feeding Candy and glanced at Gabe. "*Rethink* our party?"

"Well," Gabe said, smiling for everyone in the dining room as he squeezed Kassandra's hand. "Kassandra and I have decided we *do* want to get married right here, right now, and the Christmas party seems like the perfect opportunity."

"But it's only a few days away!"

"That's one of the things we'd like you to rethink. We'd like to move the date back about a week."

"Oh, my gosh! You mean it!" Emma said, then covered her mouth with her gnarled fingers. "You're actually getting married?"

Loretta stopped feeding Candy and sat motionless as Sam rose from his seat. "Well, congratulations," he said, and walked over to the buffet. He pulled out a tray of fluted glasses and set them on the table before he rang a bell for the maid. "Please get us a bottle of champagne," he said when she entered. "My son is getting married."

The maid smiled and nodded, then scurried from the room.

"There's so much to do," Loretta said, almost sounding as if she were thinking aloud. "I'd literally have to cancel my party...."

"And then not reinvite about a hundred and fifty of the people you'd originally invited," Gabe said cautiously. "We'd like a small wedding."

"A small wedding," Loretta gasped. "But Gabe..."

"Small, Mother."

"Then there's no reason to cancel the party," Emma pointed out logically. "We can still have the party on Saturday just as we'd planned, and set your wedding for..."

"Christmas Eve," Loretta decided. "We'll have the guests assemble at about eleven-thirty, so you can say your vows at midnight. We'll light the entire living room with nothing but white candles and..."

"Wait a minute," Gabe interrupted. "We don't want anything big or *fancy*."

"Let's hear what Kassandra has to say about that," Emma said, and all eyes turned toward Kassandra.

"Well, to be honest," Kassandra ventured uncertainly, "I definitely don't want anything big, but I wouldn't mind fancy."

"Yes!" Loretta shouted, jumping out of her chair. "We start shopping tomorrow." She turned to Gabe's grandmother. "Emma, are you up for this?"

"Are you kidding?" Emma said, then rose. "I'm going to bed right now, just to make sure I am ready for it."

"But you haven't had champagne," Sam protested as she started out of the room.

"Honey, I don't need champagne. That announcement left me punch-drunk. I'll see you people in the morning."

* * *

When Gabe's parents finally took Candy up to her room about an hour later, Gabe breathed a giant sigh of relief. "Well," he said, tugging on his tie. "I'd say we salvaged everything."

"I'd say we did," Kassandra agreed, then settled on the white leather sofa in the living room.

"You were right about knowing they'd believe the plan much more if you contradicted me about the fancy wedding."

"That was the only concession I knew we could make that would assure they'd let us keep the wedding small. I knew if we insisted on having things too different from the wedding they'd always envisioned for you, they'd start fighting us and pretty soon one of us would slip about something."

"Yeah, well, whatever your reasoning, it worked," Gabe said, and started toward the bar. "Can I get you a drink?"

"I really think I could use a drink right now," Kassandra admitted softly.

Shaking his head, Gabe chuckled. "I know exactly what you mean. White wine?"

"White wine is fine. After all, we've still got hours and hours of figuring to do. Anything stronger and I'd fall asleep."

Gabe poured two glasses of wine and joined her on the sofa. "I'm not quite sure what else you think we need to figure out. The way it seems to me, my mother and grandmother would be happy to take it from here, and all we'd have to do is sit back and enjoy the ride."

"Not hardly," Kassandra said. She took a small sip of her wine, let it linger on her tongue, then swallowed. "They may plan most of the wedding, but we're not exactly out of the picture yet. First we still have ruffled feathers to smooth about not using the minister from your parents' church. And also we didn't talk them out of the Christmas party, which means you and I will be facing two hundred of your parents' dearest friends on Saturday. And each and every one of them will not only expect to hear a few dating stories, most of them will want to hear bits and pieces of my past. We're either going to have to make up a good story that you can remember, or I'm going to have to tell you enough about myself that you can sound like an expert before Saturday.''

''I think you're right,'' Gabe agreed. He set his wine on the coffee table, leaned back on the couch and closed his eyes. ''I'm ready. Fill me in on the story of your life. The *real* story of your life. This way at least one of us will always know the actual facts.'' Opening his eyes, he turned his head so he could see her. ''Make it the abridged version, of course.''

Tired, but resigned, Kassandra said, ''Well, I told you all the important things at the diner the first night we were here. Now we have to get into the dull, nitty gritty things like grade school teachers and high school friends.''

Gabe chuckled, settling in on the sofa again. ''That's fine. Great, actually. Those things will give our story character.''

''Yes, but because my life is mostly dull, that also means people will see there's less reason for you to have fallen in love with me.''

He laughed again. ''Not really. Physically you've got enough good reason going on that I wouldn't need any more encouragement than how you look.''

''You're that shallow?''

He opened his eyes again. ''No, you're that good-looking.'' Seeing her seemed to resurrect a memory and he smiled. ''I'll tell you what. All you need to do is buy something red to wear to the party. You looked spectacular in that red jumpsuit the other night. You wear that or something like that and I can guarantee no one will question why I decided to marry you.''

Heat coursed through her limbs, but Kassandra ignored it. She didn't really want to be pleased by his compliment, but she was, and she couldn't deny it. Still, she didn't want

Gabe to know that. If he ever realized she was pleased he found her attractive, he'd realize that could only be because she found him attractive, and he'd never let her live it down.

"Fine, I'll just be sure to wear something alluring to the party," she said, then cleared her throat and changed the subject. "So, why am I supposed to have fallen in love with *you?*"

He grinned hopefully. "Same reason?"

She shook her head. "I'd never fall for someone on the basis of looks alone."

"How about my looks and my money?"

"Oh, I'm sure that would impress your parents' friends and relatives."

"How about my looks, my money and my charm?"

"Let's work on your charm," she said, and smiled to let Gabe know the double entendre had been intentional. "Let's work really hard on your charm."

"You know, Kassie," Gabe said, scooting closer to her on the sofa, "if I didn't know better, I'd think you didn't like me."

"I don't. You know I don't," Kassandra said, because finding him attractive and liking him were definitely two different things. He was dangerous and daring. She was quiet and simple. Even if they wanted to like each other, there wasn't any common ground in which to do it. She subtly slid away from him. "And you don't like me, either. That's why I think we're going to have problems pulling this off unless we tell each other a little bit more about our pasts."

"All right. Fine," he said. "Let's get back to the grade school teachers and high school friends."

Kassandra spent the next ten minutes telling him everything she could remember about her distant past. He sat stock still, his eyes closed, his breathing so even she wondered if he wasn't asleep. Though she concentrated on her story, Kassandra was irresistibly drawn to studying his face, the bold angles of his cheekbones and jaw, the whiskery stubble he couldn't seem to lose because it was so dark, and his beautiful, shiny black hair. It was no wonder this charade had become so difficult for her. He was handsome, personable when he wanted to be, and so devoted to his grandmother it was endearing. Thank God she could also remember he was pushy, arrogant, demanding and spoiled. Otherwise, she wouldn't stand a chance.

"And that takes us up to my getting a job at the restaurant and realizing I wanted to teach."

Appearing as if he'd finally gotten into his part, Gabe opened his eyes, turned to her and asked, "Why?"

"Why did I decide I wanted to be a teacher?" she asked, and he nodded. "All along I knew I wanted a job with meaning and purpose. I just didn't know what it was. Then, when I realized how much I liked kids, teaching just seemed like the natural choice."

"That's nice," Gabe said, and settled into the couch again. "I like that. I think my parents' friends will like that, too."

"So, why did you choose your job?" Kassandra asked, turning the tables because she'd run out of things to say.

He shrugged. "It was expected of me."

She waited for him to continue, and when he didn't she said, "That's all?"

"Basically," he said, then, seeing the expression on her face, he sighed. "Hey, my job gives my life meaning and purpose, too."

"Really?" she asked, truly curious now.

"Of course," he said, then he laughed. "If it didn't, Kassie, do you really think I'd keep it?"

She thought about that, then shook her head. "No, I don't suppose you would."

Triumphant, he smiled. "See, you're starting to know me already."

Pleased with their progress, Kassandra also smiled. "I guess I am."

Unfortunately, he seemed to take that smile as more than she intended and moved closer to her. "There really isn't too much more for us to figure out about each other. You know I'm stubborn and determined, yet committed and honest. All the things I genuinely believe a future teacher would think would make a good husband."

"Hmm," Kassandra said, and scooted away from him.

He slid beside her again. "And you're all the things I think a good wife should be. Caring, intelligent, a great mother... and beautiful and incredibly exciting."

That got her attention, and she stopped trying to get away from him. "You think I'm exciting?" she asked skeptically.

"Kassie, you never hesitated to yell at the man who owns your building. That in and of itself makes you exciting... challenging," he added, then smiled wickedly.

"Wait a minute," she said, bouncing off the couch. "Don't even start seeing me as a challenge."

"Why not?" he asked, and spread his arms across the back of the sofa again. "Afraid?"

"Afraid of what?" she mocked.

"Me," he supplied simply. "Or maybe you and me... or maybe what happens to us when we kiss."

"What happens to us when we kiss is irrelevant."

"No," Gabe said, then sprang from the couch so quickly Kassandra didn't even realize he was about to move. He put his hands on her shoulders and slid them down her upper arms to her wrists, then back up again. "What happens to us when we kiss is exciting, spontaneous and arousing. But definitely not irrelevant."

"Look..." Kassandra said, something akin to fear bubbling in her stomach. He was right. What happened between them when they kissed was exciting, spontaneous and arousing. Not only that but she found him attractive. If he kissed her right now, she wouldn't be able to maintain the facade that she was indifferent to this whole situation. No matter what the cost, no matter what he said, or what he did, she had to keep him from kissing her.

"You told me there'd be no strings attached to this. You said all I had to do is come down here with you and pretend to be your fiancée for a few weeks. You can't pick now to choose not to play by the rules."

"Relax," Gabe said, then ran his fingers through his hair. He wasn't quite sure why, but he couldn't forget what she tasted like, how she felt in his arms, and he wanted more. He knew all this had to end when they returned north. In fact, he would see to it that it ended when they returned to Pennsylvania. But for now he didn't think it could hurt anything to enjoy the moment.

But when she stared at him as if kissing him were the most frightening, repugnant idea on the face of the earth, Gabe got a stab of something he didn't quite recognize. It wasn't exactly anger. It certainly wasn't jealousy. It was something he couldn't define or describe, and something that definitely merited more thought before this kissing idea went any further. "You're right. We'll play by the rules." He turned to leave the living room, then pivoted toward her again.

"I hope you don't plan on bringing out that facial expression in front of my family. And particularly not in front of Candy. I swear you'd scare the devil out of her. Lord knows, you've put the fear of God in me."

Chapter Eleven

The next morning, when Gabe kissed Kassandra good-bye, she was very careful to be cheerful and happy. She didn't know what he'd seen in her expression the night before, but whatever it was, she wasn't giving him the chance to see it again. First, because he was right. She should be more aware of her reactions around his family. Second, because she was afraid that if he discovered that look was a cover for the fact that she was panicking over having to kiss him, he'd know his kisses affected her a great deal more than she'd led him to believe.

After accepting Gabe's chaste kiss on her cheek, Kassandra faced the breakfast table again and found Emma gazing at her shrewdly. "Because Loretta's got to be fussing with her Christmas party this morning, you and I are on our own."

"Oh," Kassandra said, not quite sure why she had a feeling being alone with Emma wasn't good news. "What are our plans?"

"This and that," Emma said with a shrug. "Loretta would kill us if we made any actual wedding arrangements without her. So, I directed one of the staff to go out and buy all the bridal magazines he could find." With that she bent and retrieved the stack of magazines. "I figured we could take these into the family room and work on the nonessentials like china patterns."

"That sounds wonderful," Kassandra agreed, rising from her chair. "We'll settle Candy in the playpen with some toys and go over those things with a fine-tooth comb."

"Hmm-hmm," Emma said, as she, too, rose from her seat.

The tone Emma used wasn't insulting, but it wasn't exactly friendly, either. The hairs on Kassandra's nape began to prickle, and she got the same feeling she got every time she was alone with Emma—the feeling that Emma didn't believe this charade. As quickly as she got that impression, though, Kassandra remembered Emma's euphoria from the night before and she told herself she had to be imagining things.

Kassandra gently pulled Candy from her high chair. Once she was securely in her mother's arms, Candy wrapped her legs around Kassandra's waist and her arms around Kassandra's neck. This morning Candy wore a white turtleneck sweater beneath multicolored print overalls, something Loretta had chosen only the day before, and she looked especially cuddly.

"She's such an adorable little thing," Emma said, walking over so she could tweak Candy's cheek. "Aren't you, button?"

Candy giggled and Emma rose to kiss her forehead. "You are just what this family's been waiting for."

Hearing the tender affection in Emma's voice, Kassandra breathed a silent sigh of relief and mentally scolded herself for imagining things. Emma was too brass and too bold to keep it to herself if she disapproved of Gabe's marriage. If she didn't like what was going on, or—more to the point—if she didn't believe what was going on, she'd flat out say it.

Feeling somewhat comforted, Kassandra followed Emma to the family room. After settling Candy in the playpen, she pulled it closer to the sofa where Emma and Kassandra would be perusing the bridal magazines.

"Here you go, dear," Emma crooned. "You look through these," she said, handing Kassandra a stack of magazines. "And I'll look through these. When you find something you like, just holler."

Kassandra smiled. "Okay."

For nearly two hours they scrutinized the magazines, gasping and giggling over the extravagant dresses and headpieces, honeymoon spa advertisements, and even mother-of-the-bride dresses. Kassandra was thoroughly enjoying entertaining Gabe's grandmother and didn't think it odd or out of place when she felt a real stirring of yearning over a certain china pattern. "Oh, my goodness, look at this." She folded her magazine pages in such a way that the china pattern of her dreams was visible to Emma.

"You like that?" Emma asked skeptically.

"Well, yeah," Kassandra said. "Don't you?"

"Yes. It's nice. Actually, it's very lovely. But what do you think of this?" Bending the magazine page around, Emma showed Kassandra a very delicate rose pattern.

Kassandra crinkled her nose. "It's so traditional."

"Hmmm," Emma said, examining the pattern again. "So it is. That's probably why I liked it."

Kassandra turned the page of her magazine and was immediately struck by an advertisement for a bold black plate with a white lily border. "Oh," she gasped. "Look at this."

This time Emma crinkled her nose. "I'd say that's a little flashy."

"Gabe's a pretty flashy guy," Kassandra ventured, and decided it was time to win some points. Just in case she wasn't imagining things and Emma did have her doubts, Kassandra knew she could win her over with this. "You've seen his apartment. Black lacquer everywhere."

"Which is exactly why you wouldn't want black dishes." Emma stopped and peered at Kassandra. "Besides, he has dishes. Red dishes. Almost exactly like that rose pattern I showed you. That's probably why I picked it out."

"And that's probably why I didn't like it," Kassandra quickly replied. "I don't want to get something similar to things he already has. I'd just as soon have him forget his past life and step into a new one with me."

"I suppose that's reasonable," Emma said.

"Of course it's reasonable," Kassandra said, then she laughed. "You yourself made a comment about the other women he dated, and the life he led. I want to put all that behind us."

"If you didn't like the way he lived, what made you hook up with him? I mean, you lived right across the hall from him. You saw it all. And, quite obviously, you didn't like it. So what the devil made you get involved with him?"

The trap was sprung before Kassandra had a chance to see it coming. Careful not to lose her composure, Kassandra smiled. "I told you, chemistry. Something. I don't know. Who can figure these things out?"

In that precise second, Kassandra heard Gabe and his father walking down the hall. He stepped into the family room, bent and kissed Candy, who gurgled up at him, then rose and kissed Kassandra's forehead.

"It's raining," he said, and plopped down beside Kassandra on the sofa. "Our golf game's postponed until this afternoon."

"Good," Emma said, pushing herself from the couch. "You entertain Kassandra and Candy while I get a nap. That way I'll be raring to go this afternoon when Loretta can help with the arrangements for your wedding."

She said the words as she was walking toward the door, and by the time she had finished her thought she was already in the hall. For a few seconds, Kassandra didn't say anything, merely stared after Emma as she moved down the corridor. When she disappeared from view, Kassandra collapsed against the sofa.

Puzzled, Gabe stared at her. "Was this morning that much of a strain?"

"This morning was fun...wonderful. It's the last ten minutes I could have done without."

Gabe knew Kassandra to be a strong-willed, tough-minded woman. In fact, he was now beginning to realize that's what turned him on about her. And now that he understood that he found her strong will attractive, he knew exactly how to prepare himself to keep from falling victim. So here he was, prepared to take on his toughest critic, and instead he found a soft, demure woman. A woman who, unfortunately, he found every bit as attractive as the tough, strong-willed Kassandra.

Gabe was starting to get the feeling he couldn't win here.

"What happened?" he asked carefully.

"I liked a set of very bold black dishes. Your grandmother said you like red."

"I do like red. I *own* red."

"I know that now," Kassandra said. "I even played right into that by reminding her that because you have black lacquer decor you'd probably love the black dishes with the lily border."

"And?" Gabe said, trying to find out if this had a point.

"And the next thing I knew she was asking me how I could have dated you knowing your history as I did since I lived right across the hall."

Collapsed against the couch the way she was, the impression of her breasts pressed tantalizingly against her soft pink sweater. Her blond hair fanned the back of the floral couch. Her pink lips were just waiting to be kissed. This was a soft, vulnerable side of Kassandra Gabe had never seen before, and though he'd already admitted he found it mildly attractive, Gabe was amending his opinion to concede he found it incredibly attractive. Arousing, actually. And he had to bring good old strong-willed Kassandra back or he'd end up kissing this woman.

"Kassie, have you ever stopped to think that you might be imagining things?"

Her eyes opened. "I didn't imagine anything."

"Well, Kassandra..." he said, then rose from the couch to get away from her. She smelled great, she looked soft, and she was vulnerable. It had been months since he'd had a date with a woman and even longer since he'd had a close enough relationship that he'd made love. And she was beginning to look pretty damned good.

Groaning to himself, Gabe turned away. Who was he trying to kid? She'd started to look pretty damned good the night he helped her with her groceries. Spending the past week and a half with her had taken her from pretty damned good to absolutely perfect. If he had more than twenty minutes alone with Kassandra being soft and vulnerable and looking so incredibly touchable in pink, Gabe refused to be responsible for what happened.

"Kassie," he said, facing her. "Don't you think it's possible that you're—maybe—exaggerating things?"

She glared at him. "I know when I'm being set up, Gabe. I mean, I knew once I'd been set up that I'd been set up, and she definitely set me up."

Frowning, Gabe shook his head. "Kassandra," he said soothingly. "My grandmother is very good. If she wanted to set you up and get information from you, you *wouldn't* know it." He paused, saw she was thinking about that, then added, "Remember the first day you were here? She only let you know who she was after I walked into the room."

He sat beside Kassandra on the sofa again. "Emma did not try to get information from you this morning. If she really wanted information she would have had it. Whatever happened in your conversation, it was probably innocent.''

Sounding confused, Kassandra said, "It didn't seem innocent at the time.''

"And you're still very nervous about this arrangement,'' Gabe reminded her gently. "Maybe you're not as sharp when you're nervous.''

She conceded that possibility with a nod.

"So you may not be imagining things, but you might be exaggerating them. Besides,'' Gabe pointed out logically, "*I've* never seen my grandmother upset. I've never seen her have even a split second of doubt about us. In fact, she's positively thrilled that we've decided to get married. She adores you and Candy.'' At the mention of her name, Candy sent back a stream of chatter. Without so much as a second thought, Gabe bent and picked her up. "You only have to look at Emma to see she's very, very happy.''

Chapter Twelve

Kassandra had been skeptical the entire time she talked with Gabe, but he seemed so intent on defending their situation she'd relented. Now, halfway through dinner, Kassandra was starting to wonder if he wasn't right. Emma was happy. Euphoric. She sat across the table from Kassandra and Gabe, feeding Candy, laughing at everybody's jokes, dreamily planning the wedding. The only person who didn't seem to be enjoying the festivities was Kassandra, and she knew she'd have to snap out of this.

Later that evening, sitting next to Gabe on the sofa, sipping brandy, discussing the wedding with Gabe's parents, Kassandra noticed something else. Pressed up against Gabe as she had been for the past week, she'd grown accustomed to how he felt, and tonight he felt different. He wasn't tense or tight, stiff or uncomfortable. He seemed very content. For the first time since the day Kassandra had met him at the airport, Gabe seemed relaxed. She knew part of the reason was that he had finally grown accustomed to having her nestled against him all the time. Tonight, she even wondered if he wasn't starting to like it a bit more than he should. But Kassandra also knew the biggest reason Gabe was relaxed was that he was very comfortable with this charade. He believed it was working. He believed he was pleasing his dying grandmother.

Realizing this, Kassandra felt a stirring of something she wasn't sure she wanted to feel. She was glad Gabe was getting his end of the bargain fulfilled; it was the reason she was glad that troubled her. Two days ago, she would have said she was glad because this meant she was doing her part, as she'd promised. Tonight, her reasons weren't quite that simple. She felt happy, comfortable and content because Gabe seemed happy, comfortable and content. Risky business for two people who made sparks fly when they kissed.

"Well, Candy's in bed and sound asleep," Emma announced, walking into the intimate grouping in the living room.

"You know you don't have to fuss over her all the time," Kassandra said as Emma sat beside her on the sofa. "I can put her to bed myself."

"You get to do it every day. Me—" Emma said, then shrugged "—I don't know how many more times I'll get to do it."

Kassandra watched Gabe's parents exchange concerned glances as she felt Gabe stiffen beside her. There was an awkward moment of silence before Gabe bounced from his seat and pulled Kassandra to stand with him. "Why don't you come to the movies with us tonight, Grandma?"

"Me?" Emma said, sounding completely surprised.

"Sure," Kassandra said, adding the weight of her opinion to Gabe's offer. "We decided to go see something funny tonight. I think you'd enjoy it."

Emma eyed them suspiciously. "I wouldn't be in the way?"

"Of course not!" Gabe said, taking her hand and drawing her off the sofa. "We'd love to have you."

"Then I'll get my coat."

They left fifteen minutes later. Kassandra tried to talk Emma into sitting in the front seat of the car with Gabe, but Emma insisted Kassandra sit beside her grandson where she belonged. Emma was even more accommodating at the movies. "To make it a closer group for chatting before the film," she said, "I'll sit behind you two."

It wasn't until the movie had begun that Kassandra started to get her suspicious feelings about Emma again. Suddenly, she realized Emma had more of an ulterior motive for sitting behind them than creating a comfortable group for talking. She was spying on them. Checking to see how they'd behave through two hours of a movie.

Because Gabe was munching popcorn, Kassandra didn't try to get him to shift closer or put his arm around her. But the minute his popcorn tub hit the floor, she snuggled close to him, nudging him as discreetly as possible to remind him that his grandmother was behind them and watching.

Her nudge took a few seconds to sink in, but when it did, Gabe easily accommodated her by putting his arm around her and letting her nestle against his shoulder. The crown of her head settled close to his chin and the scent of her hair wafted to his nostrils. He greedily sought her sweet aroma.

She certainly smelled good, Gabe thought. *And looked good.* More like the woman he was accustomed to, not that soft, vulnerable woman who had tempted him so much this afternoon. Tonight she wore a red mohair sweater and simple white wool trousers, but somehow she managed to make herself look comfortable and sexy both at the same time. And now she was snuggled up against him, shifting her head ever so slightly to skim her silky hair along his chin, inhaling and exhaling in such a way as to rub her shoulder on his chest, cuddling into him as if they really were a match made in heaven.

Which they weren't, he assured himself for the hundredth time that night. Not only were they total and complete opposites, but when they returned home, Gabe wanted to be able to get out of this relationship as quickly and cleanly as possible. Still, one night, one movie's worth of snuggling, really couldn't hurt anything...could it? Of course not. He pulled her more tightly against him.

Kassandra almost stiffened, but caught herself. This night of snuggling was a necessary evil. Her continued fear over his grandmother's odd behavior seemed to be driving her right into Gabe's arms, and lately those arms were starting to feel like a safe haven. Which was absurd. Not only were they opposites, but she, too, wanted a quick, clean break from this relationship when they returned home. But, oh, it just felt like heaven to sit like this, nestled together, not a care in the world—except for convincing Gabe's grandmother—which was exactly why they were snuggling.

It had been a long time since she'd felt safe in a man's arms, and it was ridiculous to feel safe in Gabe's. They both knew what happened when they kissed; snuggling like this couldn't be anything but trouble....

Except that his grandmother was watching. And, so what if it felt good? What could it hurt to enjoy an hour or two of feeling safe and secure...even loved? It couldn't hurt anything, Kassandra decided, and placed her hand on Gabe's chest, lending a little more authenticity to the cuddle. Gabe responded by pulling her closer. Kassandra's hand slipped beneath the opening of his V-neck sweater, across the stubbly material of his oxford-cloth shirt.

His hand slid down her arm. Her hand glided over to brush the tip of his collar. His hand drifted up her biceps again. She pressed her cheek against his shoulder, skimming her hair against his chin.

"All right. All right," Emma whispered loudly. "Stop it or I'm pouring my Coke on your heads."

Kassandra and Gabe broke apart like guilty teenagers, but Gabe recovered quickly. "Be quiet and watch the movie,

Grandma," he said, smiling. Then he pulled Kassandra against him again.

But reality had intruded and Kassandra knew they were inching toward trouble when the whole scenario started again. Her head tilted to his shoulder. His chin bumped against her hair. His hand slid down her biceps. Her hand rested against his chest. His hand glided up her arm again, but this time the tips of his fingers inadvertently grazed the side of her breast. She knew the move was unintentional because she felt a jerk in his breathing, something equated more with surprise than reaction. Though she knew both of them had had a reaction. She looked up just as he looked down. A tangible sexual electricity passed between them. Without a word, Gabe rose.

"I've already seen this," he whispered to his grandmother as he yanked Kassandra from her seat. "I think we should go home."

"No. Let's go for doughnuts," Emma said, her voice booming throughout the theater. "I don't feel like sitting through a movie, but I certainly wouldn't turn away a cream-filled doughnut right now."

"Then doughnuts it is."

The conversation about doughnuts got them out of the theater and through the lobby. When they stepped out into the chilly night air, Kassandra automatically wrapped her blazer more tightly around her. Seeing this, Gabe seemed to debate for a second, but put his arm around her shoulders and began walking down the street.

"That doughnut place is around here somewhere," Emma said, not even struggling to keep up with Gabe's brisk pace. "I remember your grandfather used to take me for doughnuts. Every Sunday after church." She paused, glancing around. "Our church is around here somewhere, isn't it?"

"Two blocks that way," Gabe agreed. "And the dough-nut shop's right there," he added pointing down the street about a block.

"Oh, pretty lights," Emma said, commenting on the bright neon sign that led customers to the shop. "I guess only seeing this building in the daylight I missed that."

Hearing Emma's chatter filled Kassandra with the sense that everything was fine. There was nothing to worry about. But even as she thought the last she felt the rub of Gabe's sweater against her side and heat radiated to every part of her body.

She had plenty to worry about.

Chapter Thirteen

"Okay. The way I see this," Loretta said, sounding very much like a general marshaling her troops, "is that once we get the Christmas party out of the way tonight, there shouldn't be a problem with planning this wedding."

Emma and Kassandra sat on the white sofa in the living room, while Loretta sat across from them on one of two white brocade Queen Anne chairs beyond the round cherrywood coffee table. The house had been cleaned to perfection, but—around and behind the women chatting in the comfortable conversation grouping—servants arranged Christmas decorations and placed baskets of fresh flowers.

"Gabe helped me whittle our guest list down to a hundred, which makes this wedding nothing more than a slightly large, very elaborate dinner party." Pausing, Loretta glanced up from her list and at Kassandra. "Are you sure there isn't anyone you want to invite, Kassandra?"

Kassandra shrugged. "Not too many people want to leave their families on Christmas Eve. All my relatives and friends live in Pennsylvania, and Gabe and I have our hearts set on getting married here in Georgia on Christmas Eve. So, no. There's no one I want to invite."

"Not even your brothers?"

Emma suddenly came to life. "You have brothers?"

"Four," Loretta announced proudly before Kassandra could answer. "Can you imagine that, being the only girl in a house full of boys?"

"Actually, it answers some questions," Emma said, looking at Kassandra astutely.

Loretta didn't seem to notice, though Kassandra got a nervous feeling in the pit of her stomach again.

"You've called your brothers and they don't want to come?" Loretta asked Kassandra.

"They're all married, and they all have children. I wouldn't want them to disrupt their children's Christmas."

"And your parents?" Emma asked.

Kassandra opened her mouth to answer, but realized she didn't have an excuse to cover this one. Emma and Loretta already knew she was the only daughter in a house full of boys. Every woman in the world would recognize Kassandra's mother had longed for her daughter's wedding day. There wasn't any possible reason Ginger O'Hara wouldn't want to come. Which meant there was no way around this. Kassandra had to lie. "They'll be arriving on the twenty-third," Kassandra said, her mouth dry and tight and feeling as if it were filled with hundreds of cotton balls.

"Really," Emma drawled, even as Loretta grabbed a tablet and started scribbling notes.

"Well, that settles that. We'll put Kassandra's parents in the green guest room and Albert and Muriel can get a hotel."

"That will make things interesting," Emma said, rising from her seat.

"Albert and Muriel will just have to understand," Loretta began, but Kassandra interrupted her.

"Oh, please, don't take someone else's room for my parents," Kassandra said. There was no way in hell her parents would be arriving on the twenty-third, because Kassandra hadn't invited them. In fact, she hadn't even told them about the wedding, although her mother did know about the charade. Kassandra knew that before the twenty-third she would have to think of a lie to cover this lie, but for the moment she was more concerned with keeping the sleeping arrangements intact so that her parents' absence wouldn't be so obvious. "I'm sure they'll be happy to stay at a hotel."

"Oh, no," Emma cooed. "Don't be silly, dear. We want them here."

"Absolutely," Loretta concurred, though her tone was definitely different from Emma's. Loretta sounded soft and sweet, generous and accommodating, while Emma sounded like a mad scientist ready to get her next victim. The only thing she didn't do was rub her hands together with glee.

"It's time for the baby to get up from her nap," Emma said as she walked to the living room door. When she turned to face Kassandra and Loretta again, her expression was one of devilish delight. "Don't plan anything without me. I don't want to miss a minute of this."

Damn it! Kassandra thought. She wasn't wrong. Emma was onto them—onto this scheme of theirs—and she was enjoying making them suffer. Kassandra's thoughts stopped and she backed up about two paces. Emma wasn't making *them* suffer. She was only making Kassandra suffer. Why? Because Kassandra was the weak link in this charade. Emma knew Gabe was too tough, too smart to crack under pressure, but Kassandra was something like an unknown factor. At this point, Emma might only suspect chicanery, and feel that the quickest, easiest way to flush them out was by hammering away at the weak link. She didn't say anything in front of Gabe just in case the scheme wasn't a scheme, but a real engagement. But she definitely, absolutely, posi-

tively, took advantage of every opportunity to catch Kassandra off guard and try to cause her to make a mistake.

Knocked slightly off balance by this revelation, Kassandra leaned back on the couch. The fate of this entire charade rested on her shoulders. Gabe wasn't going to slip up
because Emma wasn't testing him. But Kassandra could slip
up because she was under constant scrutiny. That meant she
had to be on her toes at all times.

All times.

She had to think, act, talk, live, eat, sleep the fantasy of
marrying Gabriel Cayne.

Even as she thought the last, Kassandra's heart tightened. It wouldn't take too much of a stretch of the imagi-
nation to believe she was in love with Gabe. It wouldn't take
too much of a stretch to behave as if she were in love with
him. Those were the simple things. He looked great, he
smelled like heaven, he treated her as if she were the most
important person on the face of the earth—when his
grandmother was around.

The hard part would be getting out of this mess with her
heart intact, because the longer she was around him and the
more she pretended to be in love with him, the more she was
starting to believe their lie. Not because she loved Gabe, but
because she *could* love the man he pretended to be for his
grandmother.

The night of the Christmas party, Kassandra pressed her
hand to her stomach in the hope of quieting the butterflies
dancing through her middle. In her few minutes of private
time this afternoon, she'd concluded that it was possible to
be so thoroughly convincing that Emma didn't have a doubt
in her mind, even as Kassandra kept herself from getting so
caught up in the charade she started imagining things—
feelings—that weren't there. All Kassandra had to do was
pour her heart and soul into playing the adoring fiancée
whenever there was anyone around. Then, when she and

Gabe were alone, she would use an equal amount of fervor and energy reminding herself that Gabe was the inconsiderate bachelor who lived across the hall and made her life miserable.

Simple. No problem.

So why were her hands trembling? she thought as Gabe's light knock sounded on her door.

He didn't wait for her to admit him, because they'd determined almost immediately that Emma would see that as a dead giveaway to the fact that they weren't intimate, which they should be. Kassandra had told him to knock and then enter, and they'd deal with the consequences later. Thus far there hadn't been any consequences, because knowing he could simply walk in at any time had kept Kassandra prepared. But tonight, even fully dressed and ready for him, Kassandra's butterflies took flight as the door opened and Gabe stepped inside her room.

He looked spectacular in a black tuxedo. Black studs stood out against his white shirt and matched his slightly larger cuff links. All of which highlighted his dark hair and dark eyes.

"You look really good," she said, the words coming out of her mouth before she could weigh them for meaning.

"You look really good, too," he said, obviously suffering from the same lapse of caution that she had. "That dress is absolutely gorgeous."

Glad for the break in the potentially dangerous conversation, Kassandra glanced down at her deep purple velvet dress and said smugly, "You would be shocked at what I paid for it."

Gabe smiled. "Actually, I'd love to know. I've never known anyone who bought anything on sale before. I'm very impressed that you could buy something so beautiful for so little. It makes you seem so clever."

"I am clever," Kassandra said, ignoring the warm rush of feeling his compliment gave her. This was one of those times she was supposed to remind herself of how he behaved in Pennsylvania so she could avoid reactions like rushes of pleasure when he was around. She stiffened, gave her bouncy nest of yellow curls a quick fluff, then turned to face him. "Let's go," she ordered abruptly.

Her brusque tone seemed to bring him back to reality. "Yes, Your Highness," he said, opening the door for her and motioning her to precede him.

"Where's Candy?" he asked as they strode down the hall like two executives on their way to a board meeting, rather than two people about to announce their engagement at a Christmas party.

"Isabelle is keeping her tonight," Kassandra said, referring to the Cayne's live-in maid. "Though I suspect your mother might have Candy make one appearance for the benefit of any of her friends who may not have met Candy yet."

Gabe shook his head in wonder. "My parents absolutely adore Candy."

"Yes, I know," Kassandra said. Thinking of how hard the separation would be on Gabe's parents, Kassandra knew her voice came out a little more harsh than she intended.

"That's not a crime," Gabe said angrily.

"No, but it is a problem," Kassandra said, then stopped Gabe at the top of the stairway. "And it's also not something we want to be discussing out in the open like this," she added, indicating the wide, exposed corridor.

For several seconds Gabe only stared at her. She watched an array of emotions ranging from confusion to anger skitter across his face. When he sighed, Kassandra knew it was to release some of his fury so it wouldn't come out in his words. "Anything else you'd like to remind me before we go downstairs and try to convince two hundred people that we're madly in love?"

But he didn't wait for an answer. Instead, he pivoted away from her and bounded down the steps, leaving her to enter the Cayne's living room, and their Christmas party, on her own.

Racing down the steps, Kassandra prayed Emma didn't see Gabe enter the living room by himself. If she did, Kassandra would have no hope of escaping this party without Emma hounding her.

Chapter Fourteen

Kassandra scrambled after Gabe. He was mad enough to ruin their charade, and she couldn't let that happen. Not merely because she knew Emma was lying in wait for just such a problem as they were having right now, but also because Kassandra had no idea why Gabe was so angry.

Whatever his reason, she wasn't letting him throw almost two weeks of acting—damned good acting, not to mention struggling and quick thinking—out the window with one careless move. If he really thought about this and wanted to end the charade, that was his business, but she wouldn't let him ruin it because he was mad.

Kassandra caught up with Gabe only two feet inside the living room door. Realizing he'd waited for her, Kassandra knew he might be annoyed with her but he wasn't so foolish as to destroy their charade. Mentally, she breathed a sigh of relief, but she also tucked away the incident for future consideration. She wouldn't—couldn't—let this happen again.

"Gabe, darling," she said, sliding her arm inside the niche created by his elbow. "Your parents are over by the fireplace. Let's go let them know we're here."

As she said the last, she looked up at Gabe, and he saw her expression was one of complete, sweet innocence. Her green eyes shimmered, their color turned almost aqua because of the purple velvet dress she wore. The soft, supple material of the garment clung to her hourglass figure and caused his mouth to go dry, just as Gabe was sure the mouth of every able-bodied man in the room would go dry the second they saw her. She'd pulled her thick blond hair into a loose, curly ponytail that made her look like a Greek goddess. Beautifully regal. Sophisticated. Clever.

So how in the devil could she turn to him with those incredible eyes and manage to look innocent—particularly since she'd not two minutes before made him mad as hell?

In fact, he still felt like spitting nails. He knew this was only playacting. He knew this whole charade had to end when they went home—hell, he wanted it to end when they went home. She wasn't in any kind of danger with him. And it bugged the life out of him when she turned cold and snotty right before his very eyes, using that demeanor as some kind of safety shield, as if she needed protection from him.

Which she did not, he assured himself as he patted her soft hand. He was not—absolutely not—interested in her. Just because he'd made the mistake of trying to kiss her once when it wasn't necessary didn't mean he liked her. No matter what she thought.

"Yes," he said, smiling down at her. He could play this game as well as anybody. Hell, he'd invented this game. She was the unwilling participant. "We'll let my parents know we've arrived, then I'll introduce you around."

They approached the fireplace, and Gabe watched his father hold out his hands to grasp Kassandra's. "Kassandra, dear," he said. "You look absolutely stunning." His words came out slowly and with a kind of reverence that grated on Gabe's nerves like steel wool on Teflon. Still, he didn't lose his cool. So what if she'd be amazingly vain from compliments by the time the party was over? It didn't matter. He could handle her. Besides, getting compliments on his future wife was a good thing, not a bad thing. A real engaged man would be thrilled to have this woman on his arm.

"Yes, she does look radiant, doesn't she?" Gabe said, sliding his arm across her shoulders. He pulled her close and got a torturous whiff of her cologne. Stiffening, he started to count to three hundred. He could handle this.

"The Mankmyers, Garleskys and Bilaks are all over there, Gabe," Loretta whispered. "Start with them and sort of work the room."

"I know how to do this, Mother," Gabe groused.

"I don't," Kassandra said, smiling up at him again. His heart thumped. How could she look so sweet, so innocent, so wonderful, and be so...be so...mean to him? He just didn't get it.

"The Garleskys and Bilaks are business associates of Gabe's father's," Loretta supplied in another whisper.

"I thought Sam was retired?" Kassandra asked.

"Well, yes and no," Sam said with a chuckle. "I still invest. And I like to stay on the good side of the major players. The Garleskys and Bilaks are major players."

"So, what's with the Mankmyers?"

"They own controlling interest in the retail chain where you probably bought that dress," Gabe said, deliberately cruel because the devil in him refused to stay silent. Still, he wasn't proud of that and he guided Kassandra away from his parents and in the direction his mother had indicated, hoping that the meaning of his last remark wouldn't sink in for any one of them.

By the time Gabe had taken Kassandra on a quick tour that circulated her through the room, if only to meet everyone, Gabe was feeling like a wolf on a four-lane highway. To say that Kassandra charmed the socks off his family's relatives, friends and business associates didn't hit the tip of the iceberg. She was superb. Magnificent. An actress *extraordinaire*. And it drove him nuts.

Why? He didn't have a clue. He only knew it made him furious.

It didn't help when Isabelle appeared at the doorway with Candy on her arm to announce that dinner was being served. The baby had been dressed in bright red pajamas that looked like a Santa suit, complete with a red hat with a white cotton-ball tip. His mother immediately shuffled over and slid the little girl from Isabelle's arms and into her own so she could introduce Candy to the crowd. At this point, his grandmother scampered over and regaled the crowd with her favorite Candy stories, bragging about how she put the baby to bed, fed her and was currently teaching her how to read.

Sam reminded his mother that Candy was only eight months old and hardly talked yet, but, unconcerned, Emma dismissed him with a wave of her hand and told him that once Candy could talk she'd prove to him that Emma had taught her to read. Charmed, the crowd chuckled with appreciation and Isabelle took Candy off to bed.

All in all, things weren't going well, they were going perfectly. Exactly as Gabe wanted them to go. But rather than sitting back and enjoying this significant success, he wanted nothing more than to leave this damned party.

Instead, he took his place at the head of the U-shaped banquet table in the dining room, seating Kassandra on his right. He even kissed her cheek once he had seated her, and endured her damnably beautiful smile of thanks. He made it through the meal and through another round of mingling, but by the time the band began to play he really was ready to leave. Not only did he feel like an ass, because he didn't understand a thing of what he was feeling, but his head was starting to hurt.

"Gabe, I think you and I should dance," Kassandra said, tapping him on the forearm.

"What?" Gabe asked, coming back to reality.

"We should dance. Your parents are alone on the floor."

"Oh, yeah, right," Gabe agreed, and guided her onto the small dance floor created when the furniture was rearranged in the family room and the carpeting had been rolled back to reveal a shiny hardwood floor.

Kassandra slipped into Gabe's arms as if she belonged there and his temples began to throb. Then she snuggled up against him, resting her head on his shoulder, and the throbbing left his temples and raced to another part of his anatomy. Resigned to his own personal torment, he set his chin on the crown of her head, but suddenly, unexpectedly, she pulled away from him.

"Are you going to tell me what's wrong?" she asked quietly.

He stiffened. "What makes you think something is wrong?"

"Well, in spite of the fact that Emma is happy, your mother is beaming, and your father looks like he just made a killing on the stock market, you're behaving like a man who's on death row."

"I'm playing my part exactly as I'm supposed to."

"Maybe you're playing too hard?" she suggested, smiling up at him.

He wasn't sure why—except to guess it might be because he wanted to feel this way—but there was something about the sparkle in her eyes that made him believe she really was smiling at him, not pretending to smile for the crowd around them. Suddenly, his headache began to disappear, and he started to feel almost human again. But a small, perverse part of him didn't want her to be able to relieve all this idiocy he was feeling. She was the cause, not the cure.

"Maybe *you're* playing too hard," he suggested, then twirled her around as the music quickly changed to a waltz.

"Oh, so you'd rather have your friends and family think you're marrying a grouch?"

He couldn't help it, her description made him smile. The way she was talking to him really did dissolve his worries. He couldn't even remember why he was so mad at her before. And he wasn't quite sure why he was feeling so comfortable now. All he clearly knew was that he was comfortable, and he wasn't arguing with success. "No, you're right. I don't know why I'm behaving like an idiot tonight. I just couldn't stand the syrupy way you talked to my friends."

"Oh-oh," she said, then ran her fingernail the length of his shirt collar, teasing him, but sweetly. And, again, as if she meant it, not as if she was behaving any specific way for the benefit of his family's guests. "If I didn't know better, I'd think you were jealous."

"I'm not jealous," he said, then spun her around quickly enough that he hoped he would shut her up, because even though he'd made that quick denial he wasn't convinced that wasn't a lie. Could it be? Could he be jealous that his snooty, mean-spirited, stuffy, conservative neighbor had been fawning over his friends?

Nah, he assured himself, but he got a pang of conscience. The truth was she wasn't snooty, mean-spirited, stuffy or conservative. She had a child. It angered her when his parties awakened Candy. Kassandra had every right to ask him to hold down the noise. And, looking at her dress, he also knew she was neither stuffy nor conservative. She simply appeared that way to him because he'd never really looked....

Until tonight, he'd never really looked at her. Tonight he was looking, and it was scaring him.

"A woman doesn't really mind hearing that a man is a little jealous," Kassandra said, still smiling at him, and

Gabe felt his heart thump again. She could steal that very heart if he let her, but he couldn't let her. He had work to accomplish that didn't give him the luxury of a real wife, and Kassandra deserved a real home, a real husband. That was the true way in which they were opposites, and the reason neither one of them could get too carried away by this charade. He didn't want to live a life as quiet and simple as hers any more than she would want to live a life as chaotic as his.

He waltzed her out of the family room, into the small, peaceful reading room. "The jealousy conversation was cute for a few minutes, Kassandra," he said quietly but sternly. "But it's getting a little stale and it's making me look stupid. Now, let's get back into the party and pretend to be getting along, not fighting."

She tried to hide her reaction, but Gabe caught enough of it that he knew most of what had been happening between them on that dance floor hadn't been playacting. But she lifted her chin, lifted her full lips into a dazzling smile and turned away from him. "I'm getting a glass of punch," she said, walking toward the door. "I'd suggest you spend a few minutes cooling off before you join me."

Gabe stood perplexed for about three seconds, then he realized why she'd told him he needed a few minutes alone to cool off.

Kassandra reentered the party feeling flushed and angry. She couldn't believe she let herself imagine Gabe was starting to feel something for her just because he was jealous...and aroused. The jealousy appeared to have been something of an act, and the arousal, well, Kassandra knew that was just second nature for some men. She knew Gabe Cayne. She lived across the hall from him. He was a womanizer. And he wasn't all that picky, either. Arousing him by dancing with him wasn't all that amazing of a feat.

"So what's up, pumpkin?" Emma asked, nudging Kassandra down the table a little bit so Emma could get herself a glass of punch.

Kassandra immediately pasted her smile back in place. "Nothing. Just stopping for something to drink."

Emma glanced around curiously. "Where's Gabe?"

"Men's room," Kassandra answered, hoping that would preclude Emma from trying to find him. "Why? Do you need him for something?"

"No," Emma said, still looking around. "But you do have an announcement to make."

Kassandra couldn't help it, she let her shoulders wilt, albeit ever so slightly. "You mean, just introducing me around as Gabe's fiancée isn't enough?"

Seemingly pleased, Emma shook her head. "Nope. We get a little maudlin around here. Besides," Emma said, grabbing Kassandra's hand and looking pointedly at the third finger of her left hand, "I don't see a ring."

"That's because it's right here," Gabe said, patting his breast pocket as he came into the conversation. He walked behind Kassandra, slid his hands around her waist from behind and pulled her back against him. "We'll be announcing our engagement officially in about fifteen minutes."

"See," Emma said, beaming.

But Kassandra's mind was swirling. Not only had she gotten the feeling Emma wasn't beaming with pride as much as she was pleased that she'd tripped Kassandra up again, but she also realized this charade had become incredibly uncomfortable. Not because it was difficult to do the things they needed to do to make this plan work—like hugging— but because it *wasn't* difficult.

And it should be. Damn it. It should be. Gabe was a womanizing creep, who had not more than ten minutes ago backhandedly reprimanded her for taking this whole charade too seriously. She couldn't like him. She didn't like him. He was a dog....

Yet she couldn't figure out why it felt so good to be held in his arms. It just didn't make any sense.

The minute Emma stepped away from them, Kassandra jumped out of Gabe's reach. "That was a close one," she said, smiling gratefully at him because whether he was a womanizing creep or not, he was still her partner in crime. He was paying her to do this for him and she'd fulfill her end of the bargain—a little more carefully. "I completely forgot about the ring."

"Yeah, well," Gabe said, glancing around as if he'd rather be anywhere but with her. "Luckily, I didn't."

"Good," Kassandra said.

"Good," Gabe said.

"Excuse me," Arnold Feinberg said as he hesitantly approached the happy couple. "You don't mind if I dance with your fiancée, do you, Gabe?" Arnold asked sheepishly.

Gabe dismissed them with a wave of his hand. "No, go ahead," he said, turning back to the refreshment table. "I'll come find you when it's time to do this ring thing."

Kassandra stiffened, unwittingly insulted by the intentional snub. "Fine," she said quietly, regally. "Thank you, Gabe," she added, then allowed Arnold to lead her to the dance floor.

"I guess things aren't exactly working out as planned?" Arnold asked, gliding Kassandra across the floor until he'd danced them into a secluded corner.

Kassandra glanced around guiltily, saw no one was paying them any attention and sighed. "That's an understatement."

"What's he doing? Making passes at you?"

At that, Kassandra laughed. It was such a wonderful release of tension, she actually relaxed in Arnold's arms. "Not hardly."

"If he's not making passes at you, what had you jumping away from him back there?"

"I jumped away because he accused *me* of making passes at *him.*"

Arnold's face scrunched up with confusion. "What?"

Kassandra sighed. "He accused me of taking the charade too seriously."

"Really?" Arnold asked smugly, his wide mouth inching upward into a huge grin. "Isn't that interesting."

"I personally thought it was rude."

"Oh, no, no," Arnold said, still grinning. "What Gabe did was his classic defense mechanism move."

"Defense mechanism move?" Kassandra echoed incredulously.

Arnold shrugged. "Sure. I saw it all through college. He's got plans, he's got goals, he can't have a woman in his life—no time—so he turns the tables on her. Accuses her of getting serious so she'll dump him, so he doesn't have to deal with the consequences of having a relationship."

"That's preposterous."

"Not really," Arnold insisted. "I spent four years in college with him. I've seen it a hundred times."

"Yeah, well, I've lived across the hall from him for a year and a half, and judging from the parade of women in and out of his apartment, I'd say he's not afraid of relationships."

"What he's not afraid of is dates," Arnold qualified, then spun her around the floor. "You, on the other hand, must have gone beyond date and be teetering toward relationship. Congratulations."

"Congratulations?" Kassandra said, then she laughed. "I don't think so. First, he's not all that much of a catch. Second, I'm just about certain you're dead wrong."

"First," Arnold said, mocking her, "he *is* that much of a catch. He's a great catch. And, second, he really hasn't had it all that easy. Did you know his father has a bad heart?"

Thinking of Sam, Kassandra frowned. "No."

"Well, he does. That's the big reason Gabe gave up the offers from the pros and became part of Cayne Enterprises."

"But I thought he started when his grandfather died."

"And you believed that? You never realized that Gabe's father should be heading the company now, not Gabe?"

"But Gabe started out at the bottom...."

"Hell, yeah. And rose to the top in six short years. His father couldn't have spent another day in that office, the board of directors was pushing him beyond his limits. Two years ago, Gabe convinced his father he was ready to take over Cayne Enterprises and Sam relented. Gabe's been fighting to keep his family's company going in the direction of his grandfather's vision ever since. At no small cost to his sanity, I'm sure."

"I'm sure," Kassandra murmured. "But in the long run that's really none of my business."

"Oh, I think it's more your business than anyone else's right now."

The music stopped. Arnold and Kassandra stepped away from each other, clapping for the band. When the music started again, Arnold caught her hand. "I mean that," he said, smiling at her. "So you think about it."

With that, Arnold directed her off the dance floor and over to Gabe. Smiling like the perfect fiancée, Gabe took her hand and escorted her to his parents. As Sam dug around in his jacket pocket for the index cards containing his toast, Kassandra watched him. He really didn't look old, probably wasn't more than fifty-five, but he seemed slow, tired. She'd noticed it before, simply never dwelled on it or wondered why. Now she knew why. She also took note of the way Loretta pampered Sam and protected him. Now she understood that, too.

After only a few minutes, the foursome walked to the makeshift bandstand. Sam took center stage and made a few jokes, but he promptly handed the proceedings over to Gabe.

"Kassandra couldn't believe we were actually going to come up to the stage and make a formal announcement about getting engaged, but I told her our family likes to do things the right way. When we're making an announcement, we make an announcement. But what I didn't tell Kassandra was that my parents insisted that I ask her to marry me formally, as well. The same way my father did when he got engaged to my mother. The same way my grandfather asked my grandmother."

With that he turned and caught Kassandra's hand, pulling her forward slightly. When she was beside him, Gabe dropped to one knee and said, "Kassandra, will you marry me?"

All of life seemed to stop for Kassandra as several things ran through her head. This man kneeling on one knee on the floor in front of her had put his family ahead of his own needs for most of his life, including now when he'd gone so far as to produce an entire drama to have them believe he was settling down, that he hadn't given up everything for them.

On the heels of that, Kassandra realized he possessed the kind of chivalry and honor most women only dreamed they'd find in a man.

And on the heels of that came Arnold's conclusion that the reason Gabe kept insulting her was to keep her at an arm's distance because he wouldn't allow himself the luxury of loving someone.

The ultimate sacrifice.

Even as she thought the last, she looked down into his shining brown eyes and realized that he was waiting for her, waiting for her to help him do the very best he could by his family.

She took a slow breath. "Of course I will."

He slid the ring on her finger and Kassandra felt a very odd, very sad tingle. She would go home and throw herself back into her studies and raise Candy and eventually she'd find the right man to settle down with. Gabe would go back and throw himself into his family's heritage and his meaningless relationships. She would move on. He'd be stuck in the same life forever.

And someday...some Christmas...he'd come home to his huge, silent house, and there would be no one waiting for him.

He'd be all alone.

Chapter Fifteen

"Let me see the rock," Emma said, corralling Kassandra as the last of the well-wishers walked out the front door of the Cayne house.

Smiling, Kassandra obliged Emma's request, holding out her left hand so Emma could see her engagement ring.

Emma gasped. "It's gorgeous."

"I picked it out myself."

Sidling up to Kassandra from behind, Gabe slid his arms around her waist and laughed. "She told me the ring I chose was tacky."

"I'm sure it was," Emma said dreamily, still gazing at the beautiful ring. Then she glanced up at Gabe. "So, how much did you pay for this?"

"Isn't it your bedtime?" Gabe asked, pointedly ignoring her question.

Emma gave him an assessing look. "All right. You're right. It's none of my business."

"And it's also your bedtime."

"Well, the party's over, so it could be your bedtime, too," Emma said.

"Okay, fine," Gabe said, and turned toward the stairway, dragging Kassandra with him. "We'll go to bed, too," he said, and started up the steps, Kassandra in tow.

"I just thought you'd be more anxious..." Emma said casually. "Since Candy's sleeping in Isabelle's room tonight and the two of you could sleep together."

Both Kassandra and Gabe stopped dead in their tracks. Both turned to face Emma.

"Don't tell me you forgot?" Emma said, smiling shrewdly.

"Hell, no," Gabe said, recovering quickly. "We're just not crude...like some people I know. Good night, Grandma," he said, and started up the steps again. "And don't bother looking for either one of us at breakfast."

He led Kassandra down the hall until they reached her bedroom, where he opened the door and directed her inside. "Get pajamas and your toothbrush, because I'm not sleeping in here."

"Why can't we sleep in here?" Kassandra demanded, glad Gabe had returned to being the overbearing fool she didn't like, because it was much easier to handle him this way.

"Because my grandmother would never believe I'd sleep in any room but my own...."

"You know, Gabe," Kassandra interrupted angrily, "if you really did have a fiancée, you'd like her enough to make some concessions, to do one or two things she wants to do. Did you ever stop to think that maybe it's the way you treat me that has your grandmother suspicious?"

She stormed into her bathroom, grabbed her toothbrush and other essentials, and stuffed them into a carrying case. Then she stuffed the carrying case, her pajamas, clean underthings, and jeans and a sweatshirt for morning into an overnight bag. Then she marched past Gabe and into the hall, where she continued storming until she was standing just outside his doorway. Propriety, and his accusing her of snooping in his bedroom a few days before, wouldn't allow her to enter before he did.

"Well, I really hope my grandmother saw that display," Gabe commented as he opened the door for her to enter.

"I'm sorry," Kassandra said, though she really didn't mean it. She dumped her things on Gabe's bed, dug out the toiletries and clothing she needed, then headed for the bathroom.

After showering, brushing her teeth, braiding her hair and stepping into plaid flannel pajamas, she reentered Gabe's bedroom, looking well-scrubbed and wholesome. She knew that. She'd planned that. There was no way on God's green earth she would allow Gabe to get the impression she was flirting with him again. With this outfit she knew there would be no misinterpretation.

Reading, Gabe sat on a chair by the window. When Kassandra entered, he glanced at her, seemed to swallow hard, then rose from his seat. Without a word, he went into the bathroom.

Kassandra drew a long breath and took the seat he'd vacated. She glanced at his novel—a spy thriller—then, uninterested, set it down. Bored, she roamed the room for a few minutes, but his cabinet of trophies caught her attention as it had the first time she noticed it.

Looking at the various awards and accolades, Kassandra felt a twist of her heart again. Arnold had told her enough about Gabe's past to fill in the missing pieces, and also enough to make her really respect and admire him. But she didn't want to respect and admire him. Hell, she didn't even really want to like him. She also didn't want him to catch her staring at his mementos again, and she moved away, still drawn, but fighting it. As long as she and Gabe really didn't know each other, there was no danger that their physical attraction would escalate into something more, and she intended to keep it that way.

Kassandra slipped under the covers on the right side of the bed just as Gabe came out of the bathroom, toweling his shiny black hair. He wore only the bottoms of paisley pajamas. No socks, no shoes, no slippers. No robe, no pajama top, no T-shirt. Just the bottoms of paisley pajamas.

"I like the right side," he said simply.

Seeing his bare flesh, the dark swirls of chest hair, and the soft caress of those silken pajamas hugging his trim hips temporarily shocked Kassandra's brain into numbness, but not so much that she would let him ride roughshod over her. "Tough bananas," she said, and fluffed the pillow and got more comfortable.

"Okay, I know you're still trying to prove the point that I'd treat my real fiancée better or at least make concessions. And even though I agree in principle with what you're saying, this isn't the issue to test your theory."

For a few seconds Kassandra tried to ignore him, but eventually she realized he was right. She only held her ground because she hated the way he treated her, but this foolish issue wouldn't prove her point. It would only make her as small-minded as he was. Still, she wasn't giving in without some sign of protest. Sighing loudly, she flounced over to the other side of the bed, fluffed the pillow and lay down again.

"Thank you," he said, catching her gaze in the mirror of the vanity across from the foot of the bed.

"You're welcome," Kassandra said, and closed her eyes. But, when her lids shut out the bedroom completely, in her mind she saw the shadowy vision of Gabe without a shirt, wearing only baggy, silky pajama bottoms. Curiosity got the better of her and she opened her eyes a crack, just enough that she could watch him as he stood by the mirror combing his hair.

She'd never really thought much about men and pajamas. Specifically, she'd never thought a man could look sexy or appealing in pajamas, because the only pajamas she remembered were her brothers' flannel monstrosities. But Gabe's pajama bottoms weren't god-awful, old-fashioned, green-and-red-plaid flannel. They were navy-and-burgundy paisley and they were silk. Soft, smooth silk that rode down the curve of his bottom and caressed the bend as neatly as the palm of a lover's hand.

Knowing those thoughts were wandering into dangerous territory, Kassandra forced her gaze to rise. She studied the muscles of his back, his wide shoulders, the way his damp black curls kissed his nape. In the reflection in the mirror, she noticed that his chest was wide, muscular and covered with a forest of thick black hair. His stomach was flat, perfect.

For the first time since she met him, Kassandra realized Gabe's business suits hid an incredibly athletic build. She also realized that eight years away from college should have turned at least a little of his muscle to fat. Instead, he was every bit as well built as he'd probably been when he played football.

Which meant he still worked out. His perfect body had not been handed to him. Yet another Gabe Cayne myth had just bit the dust.

"Would you like me to get the light?" Gabe asked as he sat on the edge of the bed, ready to crawl in beside her.

I'd like you to get your pajama top, Kassandra wanted to say. Instead, she said, "If you're ready for bed."

"I'm ready," Gabe said.

"Fine."

"Fine," Gabe agreed, rose from the bed and got the switch. Using the pale light of a bedside lamp, Gabe guided himself to the bed again. Gingerly, he pulled up the cover, but he couldn't get nerve enough to slide onto the mattress. "This is ridiculous."

Kassandra opened her eyes. "Now what?"

"I can't just crawl into bed with you."

"Fine. Sleep in the bathtub."

"Well, I don't really relish sleeping in the bathtub, either," Gabe conceded with a lopsided smile.

"Then get in," Kassandra said. "Stay on your own side and we shouldn't have any problems."

"Yeah, right," Gabe mumbled, but not so loud that she could hear him. She might be dressed like Rebecca of Sunnybrook Farm, but that innocent image made her all the more tempting.

Trying not to look like an adolescent reacting to his first encounter with a female, Gabe got into bed, rolled over onto his side, reached for the lamp switch and extinguished the light. Slowly, carefully, he edged himself back to the bed.

The way he had this figured, there was a good two feet of space between them. There was no need to lie so rigidly. Not only did he not want to give Kassandra the impression that being with her intimidated him, but he also needed a comfortable night's sleep for his golf outing with his father in the morning. Again slowly, again carefully, Gabe uncoiled his bunched muscles. He let his breath out. He felt his back hit the firm mattress.

Curled tightly against the other side of the bed, Kassandra had the same idea. With two feet of empty space between them, there wasn't any reason not to lie comfortably. She straightened her stiff spine, relaxed her buttocks, uncurled her legs and rolled onto her back.

Ah, that feels better, she thought, staring up at the ceiling.

Much better, Gabe thought, his wide-open eyes gazing at the ceiling. Then he shook his head. Who was he kidding? This wasn't working... and it wasn't going to work, either. He'd never *slept* with a woman before, at least not without the obvious benefits. Yet, here he was two feet away from a beautiful woman and he was supposed to just fall asleep as if nothing was unusual.

Frustrated, Gabe rolled to his side again and punched his pillow.

Kassandra heard his frustration and echoed it in her own thoughts. Here he was, probably the most handsome, sexy, appealing man she'd ever met, and not only was he right beside her, but he wasn't wearing a shirt—and she was supposed to close her eyes and trust herself not to roll against him when she fell into a deep sleep.

Unexpectedly, she yawned. It was the most wonderful reflex she'd ever felt in her life. The yawn meant she was sleepy. *Sleepy!* Any minute now, she'd fall asleep. And when she woke up this would all be over.

Grateful, she rolled to the edge of the bed again, clutched it like a life preserver and eventually drifted off to sleep.

Hearing the deep, even sound of her breathing, Gabe envied the fact that Candy kept Kassandra so busy she got tired enough to fall asleep without much effort. He listened to her breath move in and out of her chest, imagined the rise and fall of her breasts and punched the pillow again. This was going to be one long night.

Gabe awakened first, rolled out of bed, gathered his things and got himself into the bathroom before anything happened.

They'd made it through the night with only a few accidental bumps and touches, and he considered himself saved. He wasn't tempting fate now.

Twenty minutes later, after showering, shaving and dressing in jeans and a sweater appropriate for golfing with his father, Gabe strolled back into the bedroom.

His eyes were irresistibly drawn to the bed where Kassandra still lay sleeping. Not wanting to be caught staring, he took a quick, cursory look, gazing at her black eyelashes lying against pink cheeks, the furrow in her brow, even the loose hairs that had fallen from her braid. His heart bumped against his ribs, but overall he couldn't get over how ordinary all this felt. How good all this felt. How easily he could get used to having her around. He'd fallen asleep very soon after she had, and in spite of the fact that he'd been conscious enough to keep from snuggling into her, he'd actually gotten a decent night's rest. He'd slept as if he'd been sleeping beside her for years.

Her eyes opened. "Oh," she said, stretching as she yawned. "I see you're up."

"I've been up for twenty minutes."

She glanced at the clock. "Wow! Eight-ten! Candy will think I deserted her." With that she bounced out of bed and into the bathroom.

Completely confused, Gabe watched her go. No other woman ever made him feel this way, and though Gabe knew that was a very significant, perhaps even frightening development, he chocked it up to the charade. He was growing comfortable with her because he pretended to be comfortable with her twenty-four hours a day. Hell, he'd even slept with her. He *should* be growing comfortable with her.

He waited for her to come out of the bathroom, grateful to see she'd dressed in her jeans and sweater. "Ready?" he asked, forcing a smile since he knew he'd have to be forcing one for his parents and grandmother and he might as well practice.

"Ready as I'll ever be," Kassandra said, and walked to the door.

They went to the dining room in complete silence, Gabe thanking his lucky stars that the night was over and never to be repeated because there was no need for it. He led Kassandra to the table, pulled out her chair for her and found himself sitting across from a grandmother, whose assessing look could shame an FBI agent.

"Sleep well?" she asked slyly.

"Actually, I slept very well," Kassandra said, reaching for an English muffin. "How about you, Emma?"

"I slept just peachy," she said, but turned her attention to Gabe. "You know, after I went to bed last night I started to feel really bad for being so stiff and formal about the rules of my house."

"It's your house, Grandma," Gabe said. "Kassandra and I are willing to live by your rules."

"Yes, well, my rules are antiquated. Outdated. And maybe even a little bit wrong. So, I was thinking that I'd just move into the room Kassandra and Candy are sharing and care for Candy for the rest of your visit, so that you and Kassandra can spend the rest of the visit together."

Gabe caught himself in the last second before he choked on his coffee, but it was Kassandra who had wits enough to give the right answer.

"Emma, I can't let you take the responsibility for Candy. She's a real handful and..."

"Oh, baloney. Candy will be fine with me. Besides, if she fusses too much I'll know where you are. I'll just come down and get you."

This time Gabe did choke. Not only had his grandmother sprung a trap, but when Kassandra tried to get them out of that trap, Emma wouldn't allow it.

He finally realized that Kassandra was right. Emma was either onto them, or pushing them hard enough that if this was a charade, they'd have to admit it. Well, he wasn't admitting anything. He hadn't come this far to fail.

He glanced at Kassandra and saw that though she'd kept her composure, her eyes revealed that she was playing this scenario out in her mind and not liking the outcome.

Not only were he and Kassandra going to be forced to sleep together again... and again, and again... until he thought of a way to get them out of this, but they faced the possibility that at any moment of any one of those nights his nosy grandmother could use Candy as an excuse to peek in on them.

Which meant they should probably sleep naked... At the very least in a little more sensual attire than they wore the night before.

This wasn't good. It just wasn't good at all.

Chapter Sixteen

Kassandra walked out of the bathroom that night wearing a red satin nightie with a short cloaklike wrapper. Though a sexy, stimulating red, the outfit was actually very modest, but in certain places the smooth material clung to her curves, and it was only with great difficulty that Gabe kept his eyes away from temptation.

After another few minutes of silently puttering around the bedroom, Kassandra slid out of the wrapper and into bed and Gabe gratefully switched off the lamp. But he couldn't erase the image of her standing by the vanity brushing out her thick yellow hair any more than he could erase the image of the way the red satin nightie outlined her nearly perfect body.

As he had at least fourteen times the night before, Gabe punched his pillow and rolled onto his side. Thirty seconds later Kassandra followed suit.

Twenty minutes later neither one of them was asleep.

"Maybe tomorrow night we should smuggle a deck of cards up here," Gabe suggested, then sat up and snapped on the light again. "We could play until our eyes hurt so bad we would fall asleep without any trouble."

"That would work," Kassandra agreed, sliding up so she could sit leaning against the headboard like Gabe was.

"No chance that you have a deck of cards in that carrying case of yours?"

She shook her head. "Nope."

He sighed.

She sighed.

Gabe cast his gaze straight ahead, away from temptation—or so he thought. In the mirror of the vanity at the foot of his bed, Kassandra's image taunted him. Soft yellow hair billowed to her shoulders. Her ivory skin glowed radiantly against the red satin of her nightgown, which looked like nothing more than a dainty slip with spaghetti straps. Without her cloak, only one delicate layer of material separated all the rest of that glorious flesh from ...

With a jolt, he pushed his gaze toward the bathroom door, the only neutral eye space available. Knowing he somehow had to get his attention away from the way she looked, he cleared his throat and said, "What did you do today with my mother and grandmother?"

"The usual," Kassandra replied. "We argued with caterers, argued with the florist and argued with one another."

"In other words, you're still planning the wedding."

"You're going to have a wonderful wedding, Gabe, if your mother and grandmother don't drive the caterer and the florist into a nervous breakdown."

Gabe chuckled fondly. "What seems to be the problem?"

"Well, they change the menu with the caterer at least four times a day. But with the florist they keep bouncing back and forth between an entire Christmas motif of red poinsettias and holly, or an all-white motif that would include some white poinsettias, but would basically revolve around white roses and baby's breath."

"Quite a decision."

"You'd think the fate of the world rested on it."

"I'm sure it does to my mother and grandmother." He paused, considered what she'd told him, and said, "Do you think they're having fun?"

Kassandra shook her head and rolled her eyes. "They couldn't be having more fun. I swear they enjoy changing their minds."

"They do," Gabe agreed indulgently, smiling as he pictured his mother and grandmother arguing with the caterer and florist. Then, remembering something else she'd said, he frowned. "So why are *you* and my mother and grandmother fighting?"

She hesitated. "They don't like what I've chosen to wear."

Concerned, Gabe faced her. "Why not?"

"I'm not quite sure. I've chosen a perfectly lovely white suit. I picked it up for a song because it had been hanging on the rack long enough that it needed to be dry cleaned. I sent it out to have it cleaned and now it's as good as new."

For a full thirty seconds Gabe merely absorbed what she said, smart enough not to make a snap judgment because the last outfit she'd chosen—the purple velvet dress—had been as pretty as any of the more expensive dresses at his parents' Christmas party. For all he knew, this white suit might be the perfect wedding attire.

"You're satisfied with this suit?" he asked.

"Absolutely," she said confidently. "I think it's beautiful."

"And I trust your judgment. Stick by your guns."

"You mean it?" she asked excitedly.

He raised his hands in submission. "Yes."

His answer seemed to please her enormously, because her lips curled upward into a beautiful smile, and before Gabe realized what was happening, she threw her arms around him and hugged him.

"Thanks," she said, squeezing him once, hard, then releasing him just as quickly.

"Anything else you'd like to hear about the wedding?" she asked cheerfully.

He cleared his throat. "No," he said. "I think I'd better just lie down and try to go to sleep."

"Yeah, me, too," she agreed slowly, sliding down to her pillow, and rolling onto her side.

Gabe switched off the lamp again and also returned to his side of the bed. He and Kassandra lay quietly in the dark for several minutes before he heard the sound of her deep, even breathing, indicating she'd fallen asleep.

Opening his eyes, Gabe rolled over and studied the slope of her body beneath the blanket. He had a strange, fluttery feeling in the pit of his stomach that wouldn't go away, and though he didn't know what it was, he did know Kassandra had caused it. Or her reaction to their conversation had caused it. He'd never met anyone who got so pleased over little things, or anyone who was so easy to please. And for some reason or another pleasing her had somehow gotten all tied up with sexual feelings and that sort of made him mad. Now they wouldn't even be able to have a friendly conversation again without him thinking of this night in this bed and how wickedly attracted he was to her.

At the same time, he realized that he also respected her more than he respected any other person in his life, and he—in good conscience—wouldn't be able to ignore her anymore, either.

And both of those added up to nothing but trouble when they returned to Pennsylvania.

The next day was a bustle of activity, but for some reason or another Kassandra found herself alone in the middle of a crowd. Candy played peacefully in her playpen, perfectly content to sit in the center of the action, listening as

Gabe's mother directed cleaning crews and his grand-mother gave hors d'oeuvre recipes to the new caterer.

"So, what do you think, Kassandra?"

Realizing someone had spoken to her, Kassandra quickly glanced up and said, "Excuse me?"

"I asked what you thought about serving all-white cookies."

"Oh, I see we're back to the all-white motif?"

Emma nodded happily. "What's more beautiful than white roses and baby's breath?"

"Nothing, I guess," Kassandra agreed.

Loretta immediately turned to face her. "What's the matter, dear?"

"Nothing. Nothing," Kassandra hastily assured her.

Emma took the seat beside her on the sofa. "Don't tell us 'nothing.' I heard that tone, too."

The truth of the matter was Kassandra felt very strange about her conversation with Gabe from the night before. She'd never been so pleased to have someone support her as she had been to have Gabe's approval over the wedding dress. But then she hugged him and he stiffened as if hugging her were the most repulsive thing in the world. When she rolled away from him to go to sleep, it was everything she could do not to burst into tears.

Maybe another woman would question her response or think it confusing, but Kassandra knew exactly what had happened. She hadn't merely softened toward Gabe after spending two weeks pretending to be his fiancée. She'd fallen in love with him. He was undoubtedly the most un-selfish man she'd ever met. But he was also the stupidest. He didn't see, because he refused to see, that there could be room enough in his life for a real marriage and a real family. He was so absolutely positive he was right that he wouldn't listen to another opinion. And he'd never listen to hers. He didn't even like her. He'd laugh in her face if she told him she thought he deserved better than a fake marriage, that he should try for the real thing. At least, if she didn't say anything, she'd come out of this with her dignity.

Or so she thought. How dignified was it to be in love with someone who couldn't love you in return?

"I think I know what's wrong," Loretta ventured authoritatively. "I think you're missing your family."

It sounded like a much better excuse to give to Gabe's mother and grandmother than the real one, so Kassandra smiled sheepishly. "You know, you're right. I probably am a little homesick."

"Why don't you go upstairs right now and call your mother?"

"Better yet," Emma interrupted. "Talk her into coming to the wedding."

Kassandra shook her head. "My father has pneumonia, remember?" she said, using the excuse she'd made up as a way to get out of asking her parents to come to the wedding. She rose from the sofa. "My mother can't leave him. But," she added, walking toward the door, "I don't think it would hurt to call her."

"That's a good girl," Loretta agreed. "Emma and I will take care of everything down here."

Emma smiled. "You bet. Loretta and I will take care of everything."

Kassandra noticed the peculiar tone in Emma's voice when she said that, but was too far into the hall to turn and check her expression. It almost didn't matter, though, what her tone was or how skeptical she was about this engagement. Two days from now they would pull off the pièce de résistance by getting married—or making everybody think they'd gotten married—and even Emma wouldn't be able to argue anymore.

Kassandra knew she should have been pleased that their plan had come to complete fruition, and successfully, but for some reason or another this whole charade had lost its joy.

Chapter Seventeen

Deciding that a good talk with her mother was exactly what she needed, Kassandra grabbed the banister and propelled herself up the steps. She hurried to her room, picked up the phone receiver and suddenly had second thoughts.

Her mother had been agreeable to this charade with Gabe, but not enthusiastically so. She recognized that Kassandra needed help with her rent, and she recognized that this was an opportunity that Kassandra couldn't pass up. But she'd also voiced more than a word of caution about Kassandra and Gabe getting so involved in this game that one of them would end up getting hurt. Confident that they disliked each other too much for that to happen, Kassandra had actually laughed.

Now she understood what her mother's warning meant.

Knowing she couldn't share this private heartache—or her stupidity—Kassandra recradled the receiver. She paced in her room, trying to think of a reason for being miserable and needing to call that she could give her mother without admitting her feelings for Gabe. Eventually, she decided telling her mother she was homesick was safe enough, that way she could get comfort, yet not have to divulge any secrets. But when she dialed her mother's number, she didn't get an answer. In fact, she didn't get an answer all day.

With every hour of dialing that passed, Kassandra got more and more depressed. In the space of one day she had gone from feeling highly successful to feeling like a complete failure. Not because she wasn't accomplishing what she set out to accomplish, but because what she was accomplishing was wrong. Since the engagement party, Kassandra realized she'd made it easy for Gabe to avoid the one thing his family wanted for him . . . happiness. But she now understood that in the process she'd also made it easy for him to avoid sharing his secrets or his dreams, to avoid being honest with her or himself, and to avoid actually getting to know her.

Because of that he would never love her. He *couldn't* love her, because he didn't know her. And he would never know her because there was no reason for him to get to know her. It was a vicious circle. Every time she looked at the problem, Kassandra got more and more frustrated. By the time she and Gabe retired to his room that night, Kassandra was depressed to the tips of her toes.

Gabe showered first and was reading when Kassandra slid into bed beside him. As she had on the previous two nights, she said, "Good night," rolled onto her side and closed her eyes.

Gabe said a very distracted "Good night," and Kassandra was left alone with her thoughts. She lay quietly for several minutes, but no matter how hard she tried, she couldn't console herself enough or rationalize away the situation well enough that she could fall asleep.

Suddenly, Gabe closed his book. "What's wrong?"

Knowing she'd have to respond to his question, Kassandra said, "Nothing."

"If nothing's wrong, then why haven't you fallen asleep?"

Her brow furrowed. "How did you know I wasn't sleeping?"

"You weren't doing that breathing thing you do when you fall asleep."

She sat up and looked at him as if he were crazy. "What breathing thing?"

"I can always tell the minute you fall asleep because your breathing changes. It gets slow and deep...very peaceful, and I know you're sleeping."

The oddest sensation overcame her and settled in the pit of her stomach. She'd fallen asleep before him both nights, and he'd noticed—almost as if he'd cared about her.

"Are you going to tell me?"

Still somewhat shell-shocked from her last realization, Kassandra didn't quite grasp what he was talking about. "Tell you what?"

Gabe closed his book and set it on the night table. Obviously striving to be casual, he said, "Tell me what's bothering you."

Kassandra didn't even have to consider her answer. She knew that if she told him the truth—that she felt this charade was a big mistake, that his family only wanted to see him married because they wanted to see him happy—he wouldn't understand the significance of that. Worse, he'd go ballistic if she took her explanation far enough that she got to the point where she told him the charade had backfired and she wanted out....

But, then again, she didn't really want out of the charade. Stupid as it sounded, she had a strange, compelling feeling that if she stayed with this charade long enough it would come true. That they would be getting married for real two days from now. That unapproachable Gabe Cayne would love her as much as she loved him. And that she would be *allowed* to love him—to show him how much she loved him.

But that was ridiculous—or maybe wishful thinking.

Turning away from him, she punched her pillow and lay down again. "There's nothing wrong."

He sighed. "Oh, come on. I can hear it in your tone. I can see it on your face. Tell me what it is," he said, coaxing her. "Maybe I can fix it."

It wasn't so much what he said, but the gentle, considerate way in which he said it that caused Kassandra to sit up and look at him again. His eyes were fixed on her. His lips turned upward slightly in a hopeful smile. And, just as he'd said her tone of voice had clued him in that there actually was something wrong with her, his tone of voice had her believing he truly did want to hear. He truly did care.

She shook her head as if to clear a haze. Now, that really was wishful thinking.

She made a move to turn away again, but he caught her wrist. "I'm not letting you lie back down and pretend nothing's wrong when I know something's wrong. So just tell me." He smiled again, and in the soft tone he'd used before added, "Please."

She almost melted, but knew she couldn't. They had a bargain, an agreement. She pretended to be his girlfriend, he gave her eighteen months' rent free. It was too good of a deal to jeopardize with a confession that would only serve to make them both feel too awkward to take this bargain to its appropriate conclusion.

"Please," he pleaded again, this time squeezing her hand.

Delicious warmth spread up her arm. Her heart swelled. *This,* she decided, must be what it felt like when you not only loved somebody, but he loved you back. *This* was what was missing with Jeff. *This*, this feeling, this bubble in her stomach, this warm rush of emotion just from a mere touch, *this* was what she'd waited all her life to find. Now she understood why she'd waited, why she wouldn't let herself settle for less...too bad the reciprocation she sensed was only the obligation required by their commitment to their charade.

When she glanced from their clasped hands to Gabe's face, Kassandra didn't see the dewy-eyed expression of love, but rather an expression of determination that was all at once sexy and comforting. He was bent on finding out what was troubling her. That sentiment warmed her heart, even as it clearly showed her two things. First, she wasn't getting out of this without telling him something, and, second, this barrage of good feelings didn't have to end. She had his full attention and she could keep it.

It would mean she could only give him a half-right answer to his question, because God knew she couldn't tell him the truth. But for the few minutes it took to discuss this, she'd be enjoying his company and, for a few minutes, enjoying the sensations she got pretending that he genuinely cared about her. What could that possibly hurt? And why shouldn't she enjoy this? After all, she was only seeking a little human comfort, or maybe prolonging the conversation, not seducing him.

"All right, if you must know," Kassandra said slowly. "I'm homesick."

Her answer seemed to catch him off guard. "Homesick?" he echoed curiously.

"Well, Gabe, this is your house...your *home*. These are your parents and your grandmother. We even see only your friends when we Christmas shop or go to the movies." Feeling the weight of her misery, Kassandra paused and pressed her lips together. Now that she was voicing this feeling, she realized how very, very true it was. Being in love with a man who didn't love her wouldn't be half as desolate if she at least had her family or her friends to turn to for consolation. As it was she felt totally alone. Deserted. "I never spent a Christmas away from my family," she whispered. "I know it probably sounds silly, because I'm twenty-five, but I miss them."

"Come here," Gabe said, pulling her into his arms. "It doesn't sound silly. In fact," he said, nestling her against his side, "I'll let you in on a little secret. I've never missed a Christmas with my family."

That comment didn't surprise her. She smiled against his chest, and the slight movement of her cheek caused her to realize she was nestled against his chest—his naked chest. And she was wearing only a thin satin nightie. Simultaneous naughty and nice possibilities assaulted her, then, on the heels of those, came panic. Pure, unadulterated panic. She couldn't snuggle against the naked chest of the man she loved. It wasn't merely foolish, it was downright dangerous.

She pulled away. "Well, thanks for the comfort," she said nervously. "I don't want to burden you anymore with my troubles."

He grabbed her before she could roll away from him and lie down again. "You're not burdening me," he said in a voice that almost bordered on angry. Annoyed was probably the best word for it. "Why would you think you were burdening me? You know you're not a problem to me. We're in this together."

"Yeah, I know," Kassandra agreed, feeling herself getting helplessly trapped in a torrent of emotion that confused simple human concern with individual and specific feelings, and with sexual complications tossed in on top of all that. "But my being homesick isn't a part of our bargain."

"The hell it isn't," he said, sounding angry again. "You wouldn't be here if it weren't for the bargain, which means you wouldn't be homesick if it weren't for the bargain."

"All right, you've got me," Kassandra said uneasily, deciding it was time to back off. She had no idea what was making him so angry, but she wasn't going to push him or test him, not when she was feeling so vulnerable. Every inch of her skin tingled. Her fingers itched to touch him. Her gaze kept falling to his lips as her mind replayed memories of kissing him. This whole situation was insanity, she decided, subtly scooting away from him because she'd never felt so sexually drawn to a man before. She knew it was because she genuinely loved him. She knew it was because he was right now acting as if he genuinely loved her....

"Damn it, you're going to drive me to distraction one day, woman," he said, grabbing her wrist and sliding her back to where she'd been sitting. The maneuver caught her so off guard that she moved a little faster than he'd intended and a little farther than either had anticipated. Out of reflex, she braced her hands against his chest to steady herself, and when she did, when her soft palms fell against the rough mat of hair on his chest, their eyes met.

He swallowed.

She shivered.

But just as instinctively as her palms reached out to break her fall, his lips began to lower to hers and her lips stretched to meet his.

"We really shouldn't be doing this," she whispered in the last second before their mouths met. But even as she said the words, she knew the inevitability of making love with him. Something very strange had taken control of her from the second he started asking the questions that made her think he cared about her. Though she'd never experienced it before, she knew it was passion. And because it was so unique, so wonderful, she despaired that she'd never feel it again. Part of her wasn't a hundred percent sure she *wanted* to feel this overwhelming burst of emotion with another man.

It was too special, too perfect, too wonderful to tarnish. And too special, too perfect, too wonderful to pass by.

Kassandra knew that they were reaching the point of no return after Gabe started raining nibbling kisses along the column of her throat. She took a shuddering breath and, nonetheless, allowed herself the luxury of gliding her hands along his shoulders, down his back, across his chest. Her physical response to touching him was so potent, so intense, she felt herself sinking into oblivion. Her brain seemed to click off while every nerve ending in her body came to life. Colors seemed brighter, kisses more desperate, touches more trenchant. Until one final coherent warning entered her brain.

But that warning was enough. It shocked her passion-glazed eyes open and filled her with the knowledge of how much more difficult tomorrow would be if she let this moment reach its obvious conclusion. He'd know she loved him; she wouldn't be able to pretend anymore.

Slowly, reluctantly, she placed her hand in his, stopping him before he could cup her breast.

"Don't," she whispered.

He stared at her. "Don't?"

She nodded. Sliding herself a way from him, she rolled to the other side of the bed, closed her eyes and didn't even bother to feign sleep because she knew sleep wouldn't come easy tonight. She could rationalize her behavior because she loved him. But through all that passion, all those kisses, he never said one word about love, didn't even pretend to love her because it was the gentlemanly thing to do.

There could be no doubt about how he felt about her. And as soon as she could, Kassandra was getting away from him.

Chapter Eighteen

As Gabe began to awaken the next morning, the first thought that registered in his mind was that he was happy. Really happy. Happier than he ever remembered being.

Wonderfully content, he stretched out against the silken warmth beside him and soaked in every delicious sensation that assaulted him with each move his body made. Coming more fully awake, he used his hands to guide and direct the warmth not only where he wanted to feel it against him, but also to bring it in range so that he could touch and explore.

He took a long, slow breath, then exhaled leisurely, delirious—almost drunk—with pleasure. But as consciousness crept upon him and his hands drifted higher, he realized the silkiness he felt was warm, smooth skin. His hands glided over the swell of breasts, then the hard nubs of nipples, and his eyes sprang open.

Holy cow! He'd inadvertently slipped his hand beneath her nightie!

Gabe jerked his hand away, and Kassandra stirred, alerting him to the fact that if he wasn't more careful she'd awaken and he'd have to explain why she was on her side, curved into the shape of his body.

Gabe slid out of bed and tiptoed to the shower.

Under the spray of water, memory demons haunted him. He didn't know how they rolled together last night, but it didn't surprise him that they had. He'd never before felt about a woman the way he felt about Kassandra. He deliberately kept emotions and feelings and too much of his personality out of all his relationships because he didn't want entanglements. Now he felt as if Kassandra knew him . . .

Hell, he knew she knew him. He didn't have any secrets from her anymore. And he definitely didn't have any emotional distance. When they returned to Pennsylvania, to living across the hall from each other, their lives were going to be a mess. He couldn't ignore her now. He couldn't pretend she was just an oddball who lived across the hall and annoyed him.

Hell, she was a wonderful, sensitive, passionate—extremely passionate—woman. And he liked her. He liked her enough that when she rejected him last night, he actually respected her for it. Though it did pose a problem with facing each other this morning and every morning...for as long as they lived across the hall from each other. Like it or not they were going to have to talk about this.

Kassandra awakened feeling delicious. Her body tingled with joyful sensations. Her muscles felt rested—relaxed and comfortable—for the first time in weeks. The pleasant smoothness of satiny sheets tickled her from the tips of her toes the whole way up to her shoulders. She felt warm and comfortable.

Her eyes sprang open. Good Lord, she was on Gabe's side of the bed!

Confused and disoriented she ran through the events of the night before and was relieved to remember she'd stopped herself and Gabe before she'd given herself completely. He

already had her heart and soul. Keeping her body might
seem only symbolic, but it was important—the last thing she
could hold on to assure herself she could recover when she
returned home. Thinking about home caused a riot of
emotion. How could she live across the hall from him, see
him every day and pretend she didn't care?

Once she quieted her thoughts, Kassandra heard bustling
and moving sounds coming from the bathroom and her
heart froze. Any minute now, Gabe would be coming out
here to see if she was awake. Home got pushed to the far
corner of her mind. Forget about worrying about what
would happen in two weeks. Kassandra was more concerned about what would happen this morning. Surely he
wouldn't want to talk about this!

Squeezing her eyes tightly shut, Kassandra tried to think
of what she'd say—how she'd rationalize this near miss with
lovemaking to him—because she absolutely wouldn't admit she loved him. After the very passionate and intense
kisses they'd shared, if he didn't lose control and tell her he
loved her, then he didn't love her. Which she knew. She'd
pine about that later, when she was alone. For right now she
had to get them both out of this room gracefully, and in
such a way that they didn't ruin their charade. The best
thing to do, she decided, would be to continue pretending to
be sleeping.

The bathroom door creaked. She took a long, slow breath
and continued that rhythm, remembering what Gabe had
said the night before about her breathing. She heard the
sound of a drawer opening and closing, then felt Gabe's
weight as he sat on the bed.

With great effort, she kept herself from trying to sneak a
peek at what he was doing to need to sit on the bed. Then
she realized he might be putting on his socks and she relaxed. But not for long, because the bed shifted and
bounced again.

Unable to resist temptation she opened one eye a crack and saw that he'd only reached for a shoe. He'd done it with a great deal of movement, bouncing the bed much more than normal, but what he'd done was perfectly ordinary. Kassandra shut her eye again. Gabe sprang off the bed.

In the next five minutes, he opened two drawers, fussed with everything on the top of his dressers and slammed the bathroom door. When he slammed the bathroom door, Kassandra knew he was *trying* to awaken her.

But she wasn't quite ready to talk about last night. Foolish as it sounded, she wanted to savor this memory a little longer before he tarnished it by telling her that he wanted her to forget it ever happened.

Eventually, Gabe gave up and walked out of the bedroom, and Kassandra felt tears welling up in the corners of her eyes. There was a part of her that understood what Arnold Feinberg had said about Gabe's sense of responsibility, but there was another part of her that believed the real truth was Gabe didn't like entanglements and attachments—that maybe he used his sense of responsibility to keep himself safe and secure because that way his life was easy.

Unless she'd be willing to promise him that she'd never make a mistake, that they'd always be happy, that everything would be as glorious as those few minutes last night had been, then Gabe wouldn't take the chance of actually loving her.

And she couldn't make that promise.

No one could.

Saddened, Kassandra rolled out of bed, showered and dressed to go downstairs. She wasn't worried about running into Gabe, he'd keep everything on the right emotional keel for his family, and he certainly wouldn't discuss last night in front of them. But for her his touches would now be real, the kisses would have more meaning, the hugs would be genuine. For the space of another week, Gabe would have everything he wanted at none of the cost, but she'd pay the price.

Taking a long, fortifying breath, Kassandra walked downstairs, attempting to lighten her gait with every step she took. When she thought she had herself fully prepared, she walked into the dining room, and her mouth dropped open.

Sitting near the head of the table, between Loretta and Emma, was her mother. Dressed in her favorite blue denim jumper and a cream turtleneck, her wheat-colored hair pulled into a loose knot at the nape of her neck, Ginger O'Hara sat between the socialite Caynes, looking for all the world as if she fit right in.

"Kassandra, dear," her mother said, rising from her seat.

"Surprise!" Emma yelped, also rising.

Kassandra felt her knees buckle. She glanced at Gabe. His expression was totally unreadable, except that he seemed to be in some way embarrassed. Embarrassed for her or for himself, Kassandra couldn't be sure. She took another calming breath, this one quieter and more subtle.

"Mother," she said, deciding that since being surprised was allowed she'd use it to cover the tons of other emotions bombarding her.

Would this morning ever be over?

"Kassandra, dear," she heard her mother say. "It's so good to see you."

"It's good to see you, too, Mom," Kassandra said, inundated with emotions as her mother hugged her. "When did you get here?"

"Last night. Late last night," she clarified as she led Kassandra to her seat. Gabe immediately scrambled to help her with her chair, and Kassandra knew she probably looked white as the suit she planned to wear for her make-believe wedding—the wedding her mother would now witness. She glanced at Gabe. He gave her a look that indicated that he hadn't had a clue that Emma was planning to call her mother.

Kassandra cleared her throat. "So, how is Dad?"

"You mean his pneumonia?" she asked shrewdly.

Swallowing, Kassandra nodded.

"He's with your brother and sister-in-law. They promised to entertain him over the holiday." She turned to Loretta and Sam. "Pneumonia is the oddest disease. Joe's well. I mean, he seems well and he looks well, but we don't want to take any chances."

Grateful that her mother hadn't blown their cover, Kassandra held back a sigh. Still, there was a part of her that didn't want her mother to witness her make-believe wedding. "Shouldn't you be home?" Kassandra asked fretfully.

Catching her gaze, her mother said, "I think my place is with you right now. There are a million things we have to talk about."

Feeling the heat of embarrassment creeping up her neck to her face, Kassandra smiled weakly. She pushed her plate away, even refused coffee when the maid offered it.

"In fact, if you're not going to eat breakfast," Kassandra's mother continued, "then maybe you and I could move to a private room and start talking right now."

"Oh, look at this. We're all finished eating," Emma said, again bouncing from her seat. "You can have the dining room."

"Yes, I'm through," Sam agreed.

"So am I," Loretta said, rising.

As if in synchronization, all turned to face Gabe. "Uh, I guess I'm done, too," he said slowly. He glanced at Kassandra, signaling with his expression that if she wanted him to stay she'd have to speak up now, but Kassandra turned away from him. How could he possibly think he was rescuing her, when *he, himself,* was the problem? Telling her mother about her fake wedding was only second on her list of things she didn't ever want to have to do. Facing Gabe, talking to him about last night, was first.

The Cayne family filed toward the dining room exit. After Loretta, Sam and Gabe were in the foyer, Emma turned around and pulled the huge wooden double doors with her as she walked through. "I'll just get these to make sure you ladies have a little privacy," she said, smiling at Ginger.

Kassandra watched her mother return the smile. She had a sinking sensation that her goose was cooked, then her mother faced her and said, "Now, what's this about you getting married? Emma called me yesterday and offered to pay for a private nurse for your father so that I could be at your wedding. Knowing you had a bargain with Gabe, I played along, but I certainly hope you haven't extended this game of yours to include getting married."

Kassandra cleared her throat. "Well, Mother..."

Ginger sighed. "You have, haven't you."

"Emma just seemed so set on seeing us married this Christmas that she almost pushed us into it. But we aren't actually getting married," Kassandra hastily assured. "Gabe has a friend who is an actor. He's going to pretend to be a minister. The ceremony will be a fake. But no one will know that."

Ginger gasped. "Kassandra Lee O'Hara! These people think you're getting married!"

"Really?" Kassandra asked, smiling. "I thought they invited you here to flush us out."

"Flush you out?"

"All along I've thought that Emma suspected this whole thing was a trick. Gabe's been telling me I'm crazy, that it was only my conscience making me think everybody could see right through our story. I guess he's right."

"Gabe might be right, but I think you're both crazy," Ginger said, obviously exasperated. "Kassie, do you realize what you're doing? *You*, the woman who refused to marry the father of her child because she had too much respect for the sanctity of marriage to enter into it lightly, is about to fake a wedding ceremony."

Embarrassed, Kassandra looked down at her hands. "There's a big difference between marrying someone you don't love and pretending to get married."

"They might be totally different situations," her mother said, shaking her head. "But they boil down to the same principle." Ginger rose and paced to the buffet. "Kassie, you and Gabe might know you're not really getting married, but all these people—his parents and his grandmother—really believe."

"All the more reason to go through with it, Mother," Kassandra said, rising from her seat. "Gabe's grandmother is sick. She wants to see Gabe married, and happily, before she dies. Emma won't live long enough to wait for Gabe to find the right woman," Kassandra said, smiling sadly to herself because she knew it was true. Even if Emma lived forever, she'd never see Gabe get married for real. Because he had everything, or could buy everything, he needed, Gabe would never let his guard down long enough to find true love. "At least this way she'll get her wish."

Chapter Nineteen

Using the excuse that she needed to check on Candy, Kassandra left the dining room. She assumed Emma and Loretta would have the baby with them in the living room and headed in that direction, but Emma met her in the hall.

"Where's Candy?" Kassandra asked.

"Gabe took her upstairs. He said he'd put her down for her morning nap."

"Oh," Kassandra said, hiding her dismay. Gabe didn't want to put Candy down for her nap as much as he wanted to set the record straight with Kassandra. Knowing she couldn't put off the inevitable, Kassandra turned toward the stairway. She might as well get this over with.

She paused outside her bedroom door, gathering her courage, but the strangest sounds caught her attention. For a minute she thought Gabe was talking to himself, but when she opened the door a crack, she realized Gabe had slipped his hands into two socks and was using them as puppets.

Candy lay in her crib, her black hair going in all directions, the tiny fingers of her right hand pulling at the sock on her left foot. She gripped her bottle between her few front teeth, even as she grinned at Gabe who was making up a ridiculous story about a dog and a dragon. Pretending his sock-covered foot was a dragon, he plunged it between the bars of the crib and tickled her belly. Candy pulled the bottle from her teeth and giggled loudly. The more she giggled, the more Gabe tickled.

Suddenly, he rocked back on his heels and stared at the baby in the crib. "Whoever gets to be your daddy is going to be one lucky guy," he whispered. His face scrunched up with a confused look, and Kassandra decided this was the best time to interrupt him.

She pushed open the door and entered the bedroom, making as much noise as she could.

"Hey," Gabe said, jumping to his feet.

"Hey," Kassandra said, and walked past him to the crib. "You go to sleep," she said, then tickled Candy's belly before she handed her bottle to her again.

Kassandra moved away from the crib. "Come on. If we don't leave this room, she'll never get to sleep."

Gabe grabbed Kassandra's arm, and prevented her from walking away. "Kassandra, you and I need to talk."

"We can't talk. Candy needs to sleep."

"Then let's go to my room."

She shook her head. "Not on your life."

"Then it's the family room or a drive in the country," he said. "Because one way or another we're going to talk. We have to talk."

She sighed. "Okay, you're right. Gabe, last night we almost made a mistake," she said, and looked him right in the eye to prove her sincerity. "But we didn't and I think we should forget about it. I've been on pins and needles since the first day I got here, and last night I was homesick and lonely and fretting about Emma figuring the whole mess out. I needed a little comfort, we got carried away. But nothing really happened. So let's just forget about it."

"Forget about it?" he asked incredulously.

"Yeah, forget about it," she agreed lightly. "You're off the hook." She glanced at the crib. Candy's eyelids were drooping. Her bottle lay beside her, forgotten. "Now, let's get out of here," she whispered, directing Gabe to the door.

In the hall outside her bedroom, Gabe opened his mouth to finish their discussion, but he snapped it closed again. He was getting exactly what he wanted. She seemed to be as anxious as he was to forget it. He could tell just by looking at the determined expression on her face that when they returned to Pennsylvania Kassandra would be perfectly happy to resume their normal, semitolerant relationship. Things had worked out perfectly. Exactly the way he wanted them to work out.

He turned toward the stairs. "I'll see you at dinner," he said, and began to stride down the hall. He waited for that moment of exhilaration to come, the sense of relief that one night hadn't altered the entire course of their history, but it didn't come. He never got a sense of relief, he never even got a *pang* of relief. All he got were sharp stabs of disappointment and the swell of an emotion that felt very much like anger.

Though she had to endure dinner beside Gabe, Kassandra easily bowed out early to spend time with Candy before her bedtime. Since tomorrow was the wedding and Kassandra would have little time to devote to Candy, no one argued. Not even Emma. Hearing the excuse that it was bad luck for the groom to see the bride before the wedding, Emma didn't even argue when Kassandra said she wanted to sleep in the same room with Candy again.

Kassandra played with her daughter for only about an hour before the baby began to yawn. She dressed her in a one-piece yellow flannel sleeper, and tucked her into her crib. Having nothing to do, no desire to seek company, and also being thoroughly rested from last night's deep sleep,

Kassandra uneasily meandered through her room. She fluffed her pillows, tried to read and eventually took a shower if only for something to do.

The irony of this was, it was the night before her wedding. She wasn't excited, she wasn't nervous, she wasn't anything. Though this was a pretend wedding, up until yesterday, Kassandra had been feeling ebbs and flows of emotion very similar to what she assumed a real bride would feel, but tonight, knowing Gabe didn't love her, Kassandra didn't feel anything but numb.

Wrapping herself in her terry-cloth robe, Kassandra exited her bathroom just in time to hear three quick knocks at her door. Assuming it was her mother sneaking in to say good-night to Candy, Kassandra answered the door.

"Hi," Gabe said nervously.

"Hello," Kassandra whispered.

"Look, I still think we need to talk."

She shook her head. "Candy's sleeping."

"Then, come down to my room."

"Gabe, give me my one night of privacy. After tomorrow, we're going to have to share the same room for an entire week, because everyone will think we're married. We'll talk then."

"No, we have to talk now."

"Read my lips. We can't talk now. Candy's sleeping in this room. And even if I wanted to go to another room with you, I can't. I'm in my robe."

"You have a bathroom in there," Gabe said pleasantly, obviously pleased he'd thought of that, and muscled his way into her room. "We'll close the door."

Happily, as if it were the most normal thing in the world to do, Gabe caught her hand and drew her with him into her bathroom. Once she was securely inside, he pulled the door closed behind them.

"I don't understand what happened between us last night," he said without preamble.

"Well, I'm certainly not going to explain it to you, Gabe."

"I know about the attraction part," Gabe said.

"If I remember correctly, *that* part was about all there was."

"No, it wasn't," he argued angrily. "There's a lot more here. For one, we're getting married tomorrow. Not for real, but as part of a bargain. For the rest of our visit here my parents will expect us to sleep together. Are we going to be able to sleep in the same bed without coming close to making love?"

She stiffened regally. "I know I will."

"What makes you so sure?" he demanded, and started to pace. Still wearing the black suit, white shirt and printed tie he'd worn for dinner, Gabe seemed incredibly out of place in the small, feminine, pink-and-white bathroom. He even looked too big for the pink shell tub.

Thinking about those things kept her from losing her temper with him. His tone, his demeanor, the way he said what he said, all combined to make an innocent question insulting. "I take it you're not sure."

He whirled to face her and almost ran into the pink shell-shaped sink. "I'm not sure about what?"

"That you're going to be able to *sleep* with me."

Gabe didn't know what was going on here, but he did know he felt like he was suffocating. He was alone in a tiny room with a white-robed woman. She smelled as if she'd just showered in sunshine, and he'd bet his bottom dollar she wasn't wearing a damned thing under the thick, fleecy wrapper.

Whoa! Whoa! What was he thinking!

"I'm going to be able to *sleep* with you again," he said, then drew in a long, slow breath. "I'm worried that we won't be able to treat each other normally when we return home."

"No problem here," she said, crossing her arms under her breasts and staring at him.

Sweat beaded on his forehead, and his tie felt as if it were strangling him. He loosened it. "Kassandra," he said, trying another tack. "I'm *not* going to be able to treat you the way I used to when we return home."

She smiled. The corners of her perfect mouth tipped upward and created dimples in her peaches-and-cream cheeks. "Gabe, does it bother you that you're not going to be able to play your stereo loud enough to wake hibernating bears because you now know it wakes up Candy? Or does it bother you that we won't be able to scowl at each other in the hall anymore?"

"Neither," he said quickly, then he sighed. "Both, actually."

"If I'm reading this right," she said, laughing, "I think you're angry because you like me."

"I'm not angry because I like you," he mumbled, toying with a bottle of cologne he found on the vanity. "I'm angry because things are different."

"If it will make you feel better, I'll yell at you the minute we arrive back at the apartment building."

"You can't. We won't get there at the same time. You'll have your car. I'll have mine. Once we hit the airport, we'll go our separate ways."

She didn't bother to remind him that her car was in the shop. She was much too concerned with the undercurrents she heard in his tone of voice. She could swear he'd be sad when this charade ended. That was the reason he was angry. He didn't want to be unhappy when this charade was over. He didn't *want* to like her. Well, she knew exactly how he felt. She didn't *want* to like him, either, but she did. She loved him, in fact. Unfortunately, he couldn't say the same.

"I think you'd better go now," she whispered, opening the bathroom door for him.

He rubbed his hand across the back of his neck. "But I don't feel like we got this settled."

She shook her head. "Gabe, this isn't going to be settled. When we decided to do this, we opened ourselves up to getting to know each other. Now we have to deal with the consequences."

He stared at her for a second. "Just that simple."

Her gaze never flinched as she said, "It is for me."

Kassandra spent most of the night tossing and turning. By the time she got up both breakfast and lunch were over, and Candy was already taking her afternoon nap.

Someone had snuck in and dressed Candy and had taken her downstairs then returned her to her crib when she was ready for her nap.

As if it were just another day, Kassandra showered and dressed to go downstairs, but at the last minute, she froze by her bedroom door.

She couldn't do it. She simply didn't want to face all the bustling activity downstairs. It was Christmas Eve, and she was supposed to get married today. After only a few more days, she'd have eighteen months' rent locked in.

And she couldn't go through with it.

Though her conversation with her mother haunted her, Kassandra knew that wasn't the reason behind her second thoughts. In the long run, this charade wouldn't hurt Emma or Loretta and Sam. It wouldn't hurt Gabe's parents' friends. It wouldn't really hurt Gabe's friends. But, it seemed to Kassandra, this charade was already doing some fairly significant damage to Gabe. Duty and responsibility, coupled with enough money to keep himself entertained, had kept Gabe from having an in-depth relationship. They literally saved him from making any commitments. The commitment he made to his family might have been his choice, but that commitment was an easy one. Deciding you loved somebody wasn't easy. It was hard. It meant compromise, adjustment, give and take. Things Gabe had never done before.

It was no wonder she scared him, made him angry.

Obviously having come upstairs to check on Candy, Kassandra's mother tiptoed into her room. When she saw Kassandra staring out at the cold December day, she stopped.

"Good afternoon," Ginger said stiffly.

"Good afternoon, Mom," Kassandra replied, and wasn't surprised when her mother didn't say another word, simply turned away and checked on Candy.

Kassandra endured the silent treatment for a few minutes, then she said, "Mom, there's something I have to tell you."

"Actually, Kassandra," Ginger said, "there's something I have to tell you, too. Since I couldn't seem to talk you out of this mess, I've called your father. In fact, Emma sent a plane for him. I didn't give away your charade. I just told Emma you were moody and upset because your father wouldn't be here for your wedding. So she sent a plane." Ginger grimaced. "I'm sorry, dear, but I think this is wrong. All wrong. We'll see if your father has any better luck convincing you than I had."

Kassandra squeezed her eyes shut. "Oh, boy! I wish you hadn't done that."

"I know that your intentions are good, but..."

"I'd just decided I was going to tell Gabe I'm not going to marry him." Kassandra said, and pushed her hair off her forehead. It would be so easy to marry Gabe, seduce him and perhaps even coerce him into seeing the good side of continuing this charade...maybe even forever. But that wasn't merely the coward's way out. It was wrong. If Gabe couldn't tell her he loved her, on his own, without being coerced, then she didn't want him.

Not even for pretend.

Not even if it meant giving up eighteen months' rent.

This was, for Kassandra, the most difficult decision she'd ever made. Not because of losing her reward, but because what she was doing for Gabe was probably the nicest thing anyone had ever done for him, but he would never understand that.

Kassandra's ashen-faced mother stood frozen by Candy's crib. "Oh, my. I'm sorry, dear. I just thought your father would have better luck talking with you...."

"Don't worry about it," Kassandra said, shaking her head. "This way we'll have company traveling back home tonight."

"Are you sure you're okay, dear?"

"Yeah, I'm fine. Just tell me where Gabe is and I'll go and give him the good news."

Ginger grimaced. "He's not here. He had some sort of errand to run and said he didn't know when he'd be back. He said he might even miss dinner."

Kassandra got a sensation that felt like a punch in the stomach. He'd gotten so panicky that he'd left her. She knew he had. And the worst of it was, she would have to wait with his family before she'd find out for sure.

Chapter Twenty

At nine-thirty that night, Gabe still hadn't returned. Though Kassandra was just about convinced Gabe had left her stranded, neither Loretta nor Sam seemed to have any doubt that Gabe would arrive at the house any minute.

Unable to bear their bubbly optimism any longer, Kassandra excused herself and Candy on the pretense of wanting to start to dress for the wedding. The happy Caynes let her go, and, after settling Candy in her playpen, Kassandra sat on her bed, sinking into a black pit of despair.

Two minutes later, Ginger snuck into Kassandra's room. "What are you going to do?" she asked, concern edging out the panic in her voice, but not by much.

After looking skyward, Kassandra said simply, "I'm going to get myself and Candy dressed for my wedding."

"Kassandra, you told me you weren't going to go through with this!"

"Yes, but I'm not going to be the one left holding the bag with Gabe's family. This was his idea," she said, hurt to the core because he'd deserted her. "Let him explain to his mother and grandmother why he chose to leave me stranded at the altar.''

Some part of her real despair must have come through in her voice, because Ginger stopped pacing. She turned to Kassandra with a shocked expression on her face. ''Oh, no'' was all she said.

''Look,'' Kassandra said, ignoring the fact that her mother had obviously caught on to what had happened. ''Just go get Daddy and get him and yourself dressed for the wedding. Then when Gabe doesn't show up, I'll cry, we'll leave tomorrow, and Gabe will take the heat when he does come home.''

''You make it sound so simple.''

''It is.''

''Oh, yeah? Then what's going to happen when you return to your apartment?''

''I may not return to my apartment,'' she said, moving away from her mother and beginning to look for Candy's brand-new party dress.

''Kassandra,'' her mother said soothingly, ''you kept your end of the deal. He owes you what he promised.''

''Yeah, well, I don't want his charity.''

''No,'' Ginger agreed solemnly. ''I think what you want is his love.''

Kassandra sighed heavily and fell to the bed again. ''Why did this have to get so complicated?''

''Who knows?'' Ginger said, consoling her daughter with gentle pats on her back before she sat beside her and hugged her. ''But I warned you that this could happen, and it did, and it looks like it got bad enough to scare Gabe the whole way out of Georgia.''

Kassandra had to smile at her mother's explanation. ''Well, whatever happened, I have to play this through or face the music for him. To be honest, I don't think I should face the music for him. I think he deserves to explain this for himself.''

"Good girl," Ginger said, then rose. "I'll go get your father dressed to walk you down the aisle, and I'll get myself all prepared to be mother of the bride. When Gabe doesn't show up, you'll have two of the most surprised, but understanding and supportive, parents on the face of the earth, both of whom will be ready to stand beside you tonight, and then get you and Candy home in the morning."

Squeezing her mother's hand, Kassandra said, "Thanks."

When her mother left the room, Kassandra rose from the bed as if in a trance and pulled Candy from her playpen and began getting her ready. She drew small comfort from the simple tasks of bathing her, cooing to her, and stretching tights over her plastic diaper. But when it came time to dress herself, Kassandra wasn't quite as together as she needed to be. So she settled Candy in her playpen with some toys, filled the pink shell tub with water and bubbles and sunk to her earlobes.

A half hour later, she was lulled out of her nearly sleeping state by a strange knocking at her door. Her first temptation was to ignore whoever it was, but realizing it could only be Emma, Loretta or her mother wanting to be involved in helping her dress, she found her nicest, sweetest voice and called out, "Come in."

Closing her eyes, she sank into the tub again. If it was Loretta or Emma they'd think it a good idea that she was relaxing. If it was her mother, she'd understand completely.

"Well, they say it's bad luck for the groom to see his bride before the wedding, so I guess I should be grateful you're under so many suds."

Hearing Gabe's voice, Kassandra gasped and sank as far below the bubbles as she could.

"Where the hell were you?"

"I'll explain that to you in a few minutes. First, I think we need to talk."

"I don't need to talk to you. I don't *want* to talk to you. You would have left me stranded here to explain to your parents where you were, when the truth was I didn't even know where you were...."

"I never left you stranded. I'm here. In fact, in another twenty minutes I'll be totally ready to get married."

"Really? Well, good for you. Because I'm not marrying you. Even before my parents double-teamed me, I knew this whole charade was a mistake." Uncomfortable under his guarded scrutiny, Kassandra shifted beneath the water to be sure the thick mounds of bubbles covered her appropriately.

"You shouldn't be pretending to get married, Gabe," she said solemnly, quietly. "You really should get married. Your family hasn't hounded you to find the right woman for any reason other than they want to see you happy. You'll cheat yourself and them if you go through with a pretend ceremony."

"I know."

She would have breathed a sigh of relief except his agreement meant he truly was rejecting her. Any sense of happiness she might have had from getting out from under the burden of the charade was completely obliterated by the fact that this was the end. He didn't want her, he didn't need her, he didn't love her and he didn't have the heart to pretend anymore.

"Well, good," she said, hiding her emotions as well as she could, though she knew her voice quivered. "You can leave the bathroom now, and I'll get dressed. Then we'll go downstairs and break the news to our parents together. My parents have already promised to act surprised."

"Oh, I'll bet they will be surprised," Gabe agreed, grinning foolishly as he leaned against the doorjamb. "Because, see, I *am* getting married tonight."

Kassandra had been carefully reaching for the terry-cloth robe she had lying on the floor beside the tub, but his comment stopped her. "Boy, you don't waste any time, do you?"

"Actually, I wasted a hell of a lot of time. You see, I've known for a few days now who I wanted to spend the rest of my life with, it just took me until today to get up the courage to tell you."

"Well, I'm happy for you," Kassandra said, then she swallowed hard. Her chest felt so tight she could barely breathe. Tears were collecting in the corners of her eyes.

Gabe shook his head. "You still don't get it, do you."

She looked at him.

"It's you. I want to marry you."

Her mouth fell open. "You what?"

"I want to marry *you*. I spent the day finding a preacher who'd marry us on this short notice."

"You did?"

He bent, dipped his hand in the water of her tub and splashed her face. "I did."

"Oh."

"Yeah, oh," he agreed, then splashed her again. "So that's where we are. I'll be willing... anxious, actually... to marry you. I even got a short-notice preacher. Now the ball's in your court."

"No, first, before she says anything," Emma said, peeking from behind Gabe. Both Gabe and Kassandra gasped. "I have to make a confession, too."

"Grandma, what are you doing here?" Gabe yelped at the same time that Kassandra screamed and sunk farther beneath the water.

"I already said I have a confession to make," Emma scowled, then pushed her way into the small bathroom. "And this isn't easy."

Gabe and Kassandra stared at her.

"Okay," Emma said, deciding to keep this short and simple. "I lied, too. I'm not dying." She paused and sighed. "Gabe, I just wanted to meet your fiancée. And now your mother's furious with me because when you didn't show up I had to admit to her that I'd told you I was dying and that's probably what pushed you so far that you'd agreed to this Christmas wedding and then panicked today and run off on poor Kassandra.''

Seemingly soaking that all in, Gabe closed his eyes and combed his hair off his face with his fingers. "This is just peachy," he said, furious. "Did you also tell my parents our engagement was bogus?''

"I was never really sure," Emma admitted. "So I kept that out of my explanation.''

"Thank God, because at least we can still go through with the wedding.''

"No. That's why I'm here," Emma said demurely. "To tell Kassandra she doesn't have to do this. We all came clean, we all were at fault, and there's no reason for Kassandra to get into this mess any deeper than she already is.''

"Well, isn't loving Gabe reason enough to marry him?'' Kassandra asked softly.

Emma's jaw dropped open slightly, but Gabe's eyes lit up as he said, "I'd say, it's the perfect reason.''

"Thank God," Kassandra heard her mother say, even as she heard Loretta draw a long sigh of relief.

"Emma, how many people are in my bedroom?''

Emma winked. "Not to worry. It's only the immediate family. We'll see you downstairs at a quarter to twelve.''

Chapter Twenty-One

Two rows of white candles surrounded by white roses and holly created the path through which Kassandra's father would lead her to Gabe. At the end of the candle-lit, flower-strewn living room, Gabe stood in front of a frazzled minister who looked as if he'd been grabbed so quickly he didn't have time to comb his hair.

Seated on the left, dressed in finery the likes of which Kassandra had never seen, were Loretta and Sam. On the right, dressed in a pink gown borrowed from Loretta, sat Ginger, dabbing tears from the corners of her eyes. And beside Ginger, defying convention—as always—sat Emma, with Candy on her lap.

But Kassandra only had eyes for Gabe. Not because he looked strikingly handsome in his black tuxedo, but because he loved her. The information was so new and so rich, she didn't want to stop thinking about it, examining it, enjoying it. She let the music of his admission that he wanted to marry her sing in her head until she was nearly dizzy from it, until her heart felt light and buoyant, until the worries of the past few days found their meaning and took flight, never to be remembered again—except fondly.

The organist struck the opening chords of the procession music and Kassandra and her father walked down the aisle. She took her place beside Gabe, thanking her lucky stars that she'd agreed to this, that his grandmother had prodded them until they decided to get married, and even that they'd gone so far as to get an actual license and blood tests just in case Emma checked up on them. It almost seemed too good to be true. More like a fairy tale than reality.

The minister instructed them to face each other, and Kassandra turned to Gabe, ready to say her vows.

He looked happier, more relaxed, than she'd ever seen him, and tears gathered in her eyes. The whole time she'd been so worried that she was doing him a great disservice by making it easy for him to avoid finding his one true love, when all the while she had been his one true love.

They said their vows, then Gabe kissed her, and the fairy tale no longer felt like a fairy tale. His lips were soft and warm, his shoulders strong beneath her hands, his heartbeat steady and rhythmic next to hers.

After walking back down the white-rose-and-candle corridor, they accepted congratulations from well-wishers, and a celebratory dinner was served. Guests mingled and even prepared to dance in the family room, which was set up as it had been for the Christmas party. But after only an hour, Kassandra and Gabe snuck away. He found her black wool coat, and she covered him to make sure no one caught on to what they were doing as he brought his car around to the front of the house.

Even as she jumped inside, Gabe grabbed her arm and dragged her across the seat so he could kiss her. Wrapping his arms around her, he pulled her tightly against him, as his lips pressed against hers with greedy delight.

"I think I've been waiting all my life to do that."

Kassandra's heart thudded against her ribs. "I think I've been waiting for *you* all my life," she admitted candidly.

In one quick, emotion-filled movement, Gabe crushed her against him. "I won't disappoint you," he promised in a fierce whisper.

Grinning foolishly, she pulled away from him. "I know you won't, but save the discussion and promises for later. All this talking is cutting into precious time. It's almost daylight already. If we don't leave soon we won't have much time before we have to get back."

"We're not coming back," Gabe said, and drove his car away from his parents' home. "At least not for about two weeks."

"But Candy..."

"Will be fine with my parents, or your parents, or the whole damned lot of them. I want to get away. With my *wife* for a while."

"You're right," she said, an odd thrill building in her chest. Not only was she leaving her responsibilities behind for a few weeks to be with the man she love—her *husband*—but she was embarking on a mysterious journey.... "I don't have any clothes," she burst out suddenly.

"Won't need 'em," Gabe said casually.

"Come on, Gabe," Kassandra said, but she giggled. "Of course I'll need clothes. We have to eat."

"We'll get room service."

"How about the plane ride?"

"I own the plane. Even if either one of us or both of us walked on buck naked, the pilot's instructed not to notice or care. Besides, even flying commercial you'd look perfectly normal in that suit." He faced her, grinning mischievously. "See. You do have clothes. So we can eat out... once. Unless we just go to a different restaurant every night."

"You're incorrigible."

At that he laughed. "No, I'm not incorrigible, I'm just in love. Finally, completely, head over heels in love." He paused for a second, faced her in the dark car, his expression solemn and serious. "To tell you the truth, it's so odd I don't have a clue about what to do."

Kassandra scooted across the seat so she could squeeze his arm and rest her head on his shoulder. "You're doing fine. Just keep saying things like you're head over heels, finally and completely in love for the next forty or fifty years, and you won't have a thing to worry about."

"Good," he said, then pressed his foot on the gas to speed up their journey. "Did I ever tell you my family owned an island?"

She glanced at him. "No."

"Well, that's where we're going," he said, and, her head still on Gabe's shoulder, Kassandra settled into the comfortable seat.

"It's literally halfway around the world," he continued, explaining a little about the island, its people and the Cayne Industries holding there.

As they drove along the dark Georgia road to the airport, Kassandra listened contentedly to his excited voice. Gabe wasn't merely opening up a whole new world for her, it seemed he was finally allowing himself to enjoy that world, too.

Maybe he had been waiting his whole life for this.

* * * * *

Silhouette ROMANCE™

COMING NEXT MONTH

#1198 MAD FOR THE DAD—Terry Essig
Fabulous Fathers
He knew next to nothing about raising his infant nephew. So ingle "dad" Daniel Van Scott asked his lovely new neighbor Rachel Gatlin for a little advice—and found himself noticing her charms as both a mother...*and* as a woman.

#1199 HAVING GABRIEL'S BABY—Kristin Morgan
Bundles of Joy
One fleeting night of passion and Joelle was in the family way! And now the father of her baby, hardened rancher Gabriel Lafleur, insisted they marry immediately. But could they find true love before their bundle of joy arrived?

#1200 NEW YEAR'S WIFE—Linda Varner
Home for the Holidays
Years ago, the man Julie McCrae had loved declared her too young for him and walked out of her life. Now Tyler Jordan was back, and Julie was all woman. But did she dare hope that Tyler would renew the love they'd once shared, and make her his New Year's Wife?

#1201 FAMILY ADDITION—Rebecca Daniels
Single dad Colt Wyatt thought his little girl, Jenny, was all he needed in his life, until he met Cassandra Sullivan—the lovely woman who enchanted his daughter and warmed his heart. But after so long, would he truly learn to love again and make Cassandra an addition to his family?

#1202 ABOUT THAT KISS—Jayne Addison
Maid of honor Joy Mackey was convinced that Nick Tremain was out to ruin her sister's wedding. And she was determined to go to any lengths to see her sis happily wed—even if it meant keeping Nick busy by marrying him herself!

#1203 GROOM ON THE LOOSE—Christine Scott
To save him from scandal, Cassie Andrews agreed to pose as Greg Lawton's *pretend* significant other. The handsome doctor was surely too arrogant—and way too sexy—to be real husband material! Or was this groom just waiting to be tamed?

FAST CASH 4031 DRAW RULES
NO PURCHASE OR OBLIGATION NECESSARY

Fifty prizes of $50 each will be awarded in random drawings to be conducted no later than 3/28/97 from amongst all eligible responses to this prize offer received as of 2/14/97. To enter, follow directions, affix 1st-class postage and mail OR write Fast Cash 4031 on a 3" x 5" card along with your name and address and mail that card to: Harlequin's Fast Cash 4031 Draw, P.O. Box 1395, Buffalo, NY 14240-1395 OR P.O. Box 618, Fort Erie, Ontario L2A 5X3. (Limit: one entry per outer envelope; all entries must be sent via 1st-class mail.) Limit: one prize per household. Odds of winning are determined by the number of eligible responses received. Offer is open only to residents of the U.S. (except Puerto Rico) and Canada and is void wherever prohibited by law. All applicable laws and regulations apply. Any litigation within the province of Quebec respecting the conduct and awarding of a prize in this sweepstakes maybe submitted to the Régie des alcools, des courses et des jeux. In order for a Canadian resident to win a prize, that person will be required to correctly answer a time-limited arithmetical skill-testing question to be administered by mail. Names of winners available after 4/28/97 by sending a self-addressed, stamped envelope to: Fast Cash 4031 Draw Winners, P.O. Box 4200, Blair, NE 68009-4200.

OFFICIAL RULES
MILLION DOLLAR SWEEPSTAKES
NO PURCHASE NECESSARY TO ENTER

1. To enter, follow the directions published. Method of entry may vary. For eligibility, entries must be received no later than March 31, 1998. No liability is assumed for printing errors, lost, late, non-delivered or misdirected entries.
   To determine winners, the sweepstakes numbers assigned to submitted entries will be compared against a list of randomly pre-selected prize winning numbers. In the event all prizes are not claimed via the return of prize winning numbers, random drawings will be held from among all other entries received to award unclaimed prizes.

2. Prize winners will be determined no later than June 30, 1998. Selection of winning numbers and random drawings are under the supervision of D. L. Blair, Inc., an independent judging organization whose decisions are final. Limit: one prize to a family or organization. No substitution will be made for any prize, except as offered. Taxes and duties on all prizes are the sole responsibility of winners. Winners will be notified by mail. Odds of winning are determined by the number of eligible entries distributed and received.

3. Sweepstakes open to residents of the U.S. (except Puerto Rico), Canada and Europe who are 18 years of age or older, except employees and immediate family members of Torstar Corp., D. L. Blair, Inc., their affiliates, subsidiaries, and all other agencies, entities, and persons connected with the use, marketing or conduct of this sweepstakes. All applicable laws and regulations apply. Sweepstakes offer void wherever prohibited by law. Any litigation within the province of Quebec respecting the conduct and awarding of a prize in this sweepstakes must be submitted to the Régie des alcools, des courses et des jeux. In order to win a prize, residents of Canada will be required to correctly answer a time-limited arithmetical skill-testing question to be administered by mail.

4. Winners of major prizes (Grand through Fourth) will be obligated to sign and return an Affidavit of Eligibility and Release of Liability within 30 days of notification. In the event of non-compliance within this time period or if a prize is returned as undeliverable, D. L. Blair, Inc. may at its sole discretion award that prize to an alternate winner. By acceptance of their prize, winners consent to use of their names, photographs or other likeness for purposes of advertising, trade and promotion on behalf of Torstar Corp., its affiliates and subsidiaries, without further compensation unless prohibited by law. Torstar Corp. and D. L. Blair, Inc., their affiliates and subsidiaries are not responsible for errors in printing of sweepstakes and prizewinning numbers. In the event a duplication of a prizewinning number occurs, a random drawing will be held from among all entries received with that prizewinning number to award that prize.

SWP-S12ZD1

5. This sweepstakes is presented by Torstar Corp., its subsidiaries and affiliates in conjunction with book, merchandise and/or product offerings. The number of prizes to be awarded and their value are as follows: Grand Prize — $1,000,000 (payable at $33,333.33 a year for 30 years); First Prize — $50,000; Second Prize — $10,000; Third Prize — $5,000; 3 Fourth Prizes — $1,000 each; 10 Fifth Prizes — $250 each; 1,000 Sixth Prizes — $10 each. Values of all prizes are in U.S. currency. Prizes in each level will be presented in different creative executions, including various currencies, vehicles, merchandise and travel. Any presentation of a prize level in a currency other than U.S. currency represents an approximate equivalent to the U.S. currency prize for that level, at that time. Prize winners will have the opportunity of selecting any prize offered for that level; however, the actual non U.S. currency equivalent prize, if offered and selected, shall be awarded at the exchange rate existing at 3:00 P.M. New York time on March 31, 1998. A travel prize option, if offered and selected by winner, must be completed within 12 months of selection and is subject to: traveling companion(s) completing and returning a Release of Liability prior to travel; and hotel and flight accommodations availability. For a current list of all prize options offered within prize levels, send a self-addressed, stamped envelope (WA residents need not affix postage) to: MILLION DOLLAR SWEEPSTAKES Prize Options, P.O. Box 4456, Blair, NE 68009-4456, USA.

6. For a list of prize winners (available after July 31, 1998) send a separate, stamped, self-addressed envelope to: MILLION DOLLAR SWEEPSTAKES Winners, P.O. Box 4459, Blair, NE 68009-4459, USA.

EXTRA BONUS PRIZE DRAWING
NO PURCHASE OR OBLIGATION NECESSARY TO ENTER

7. The Extra Bonus Prize will be awarded in a random drawing to be conducted no later than 5/30/98 from among all entries received. To qualify, entries must be received by 3/31/98 and comply with published directions. Prize ($50,000) is valued in U.S. currency. Prize will be presented in different creative expressions, including various currencies, vehicles, merchandise and travel. Any presentation in a currency other than U.S. currency represents an approximate equivalent to the U.S. currency value at that time. Prize winner will have the opportunity of selecting any prize offered in any presentation of the Extra Bonus Prize Drawing; however, the actual non U.S. currency equivalent prize, if offered and selected by winner, shall be awarded at the exchange rate existing at 3:00 P.M. New York time on March 31, 1998. For a current list of prize options offered, send a self-addressed, stamped envelope (WA residents need not affix postage) to: Extra Bonus Prize Options, P.O. Box 4462, Blair, NE 68009-4462, USA. All eligibility requirements and restrictions of the MILLION DOLLAR SWEEPSTAKES apply. Odds of winning are dependent upon number of eligible entries received. No substitution for prize except as offered. For the name of winner (available after 7/31/98), send a self-addressed, stamped envelope to: Extra Bonus Prize Winner, P.O. Box 4463, Blair, NE 68009-4463, USA.

As seen on TV!
Free Gift Offer

With a Free Gift proof-of-purchase from any Silhouette® book, you can receive a beautiful cubic zirconia pendant.

This gorgeous marquise-shaped stone is a genuine cubic zirconia—accented by an 18" gold tone necklace.

(Approximate retail value $19.95)

Send for yours today...
compliments of ▼ *Silhouette*®
TM

To receive your free gift, a cubic zirconia pendant, send us one original proof-of-purchase, photocopies not accepted, from the back of any Silhouette Romance™, Silhouette Desire®, Silhouette Special Edition®, Silhouette Intimate Moments® or Silhouette Yours Truly™ title available in August, September, October, November and December at your favorite retail outlet, together with the Free Gift Certificate, plus a check or money order for $1.65 U.S./$2.15 CAN. (do not send cash) to cover postage and handling, payable to Silhouette Free Gift Offer. We will send you the specified gift. Allow 6 to 8 weeks for delivery. Offer good until December 31, 1996 or while quantities last. Offer valid in the U.S. and Canada only.

Free Gift Certificate

Name: _____

Address: _____

City: _____ State/Province: _____ Zip/Postal Code: _____

Mail this certificate, one proof-of-purchase and a check or money order for postage and handling to: SILHOUETTE FREE GIFT OFFER 1996. In the U.S.: 3010 Walden Avenue, P.O. Box 9077, Buffalo NY 14269-9077. In Canada: P.O. Box 613, Fort Erie, Ontario L2Z 5X3.

FREE GIFT OFFER   084-KMD
ONE PROOF-OF-PURCHASE
To collect your fabulous FREE GIFT, a cubic zirconia pendant, you must include this original proof-of-purchase for each gift with the properly completed Free Gift Certificate.

084-KMD-R

The collection of the year!
NEW YORK TIMES BESTSELLING AUTHORS

Linda Lael Miller
Wild About Harry

Janet Dailey
Sweet Promise

Elizabeth Lowell
Reckless Love

Penny Jordan
Love's Choices

and featuring
Nora Roberts
The Calhoun Women

This special trade-size edition features four of the wildly
popular titles in the Calhoun miniseries together in
one volume—a true collector's item!

Pick up these great authors and a chance to win
a weekend for two in New York City at the
Marriott Marquis Hotel on Broadway! We'll pay
for your flight, your hotel—even a Broadway show!

Available in December at your favorite retail outlet.

NEW YORK

MARQUIS

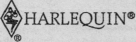

NYT1296-R

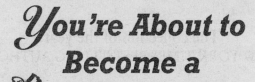